*The race is going too easily. I ɛ
jostling and fighting than this.*

A second later Ashleigh regretted her thoughts. They
were into the far turn, and suddenly everything was
happening! Foregone accelerated along the rail. A
horse was roaring up on her outside. One sidewise
glance told her it was Excalibur, and outside of him
she recognized the jockey's silks of Townsend Prince.

"Good-bye, baby!" the jockey on Excalibur called
as he zoomed up past Wonder.

She'd waited too long! Excalibur angled over in
front of her. Townsend Prince was on his outside.
Foregone was holding firm on the inside—three of
them nose and nose—with Wonder suddenly blocked
behind them. Another horse had moved up outside of
Wonder. Wonder's nose was practically between the
flanks of the horses in front, and there wasn't room to
angle out! Wonder was showing her distress at being
blocked—she was ready to climb over the horses in
front. Ashleigh was forced to check the filly.

I've lost it! she thought in panic. *I am too green. I
should have been prepared!*

THOROUGHBRED

WONDER'S
VICTORY

JOANNA CAMPBELL

HarperEntertainment

An Imprint of HarperCollinsPublishers

HarperEntertainment

An Imprint of HarperCollins*Publishers*

10 East 53rd Street, New York, NY 10022-5299

This is a work of fiction. The characters, incidents, and dialogues are
products of the author's imagination and are not to be construed
as real. Any resemblance to actual events or persons, living
or dead, is entirely coincidental.

Produced by Daniel Weiss Associates, Inc.

HarperCollins books are available at special quantity discounts for bulk
purchases for sales promotions, premiums, or fund-raising.
For information please call or write:
Special Markets Department, HarperCollins Publishers Inc.,
10 East 53rd Street, New York, NY 10022-5299.
Telephone: (212) 207-7528. Fax: (212) 207-7222.

ISBN 0-06-051774-3

Printed in the United States of America

Visit HarperEntertainment on the World Wide Web at
www.harpercollins.com

❖ 10 9 8 7 6 5 4 3 2 1

WONDER'S
VICTORY

1

DEW STILL CLUNG TO THE GRASS SURROUNDING THE TRAINING oval at Townsend Acres as Ashleigh Griffen steadied the elegant Thoroughbred beneath her. The filly's muscles rippled under her gleaming copper coat, and her snorted breaths misted in the morning air. Ashleigh looked over to the old trainer standing nearby.

Charlie Burke nodded briskly. "Okay, take her out."

Gathering the reins, Ashleigh urged Wonder forward through the gap and onto the harrowed dirt of the track.

Several of the other horses being trained at the famous racing farm waited with their exercise riders for their turn to work on the mile track. Ken Maddock and Jim Jennings, head and assistant trainers, gave last-minute instructions. From the corner of her eye, Ashleigh saw the owner's son, Brad Townsend, dark-haired and good-looking, holding the reins of his own colt, Townsend Prince.

Ashleigh knew Brad would be watching Wonder's workout critically, looking for even the slightest flaws. He was still ticked off about Townsend Prince's defeat in the Kentucky Derby nearly two weeks before. Especially because the Prince had been beaten by Wonder, his own half sister, whom Brad had always considered a loser. Until the Derby, Brad's colt had been the star three-year-old on the farm. People were looking at the two horses in a different light now, and with the Preakness less than a week ahead, on the third Saturday in May, the challenge was on.

Ashleigh could feel the watching eyes as she moved Wonder up the track at an easy trot. The filly seemed to know she was in the spotlight. She sidestepped across the dirt, tossing her head and sending the silky strands of her mane flying. Ashleigh kept a firm grip on the reins and proceeded with Wonder's warm-up, knowing the filly was ready to go at the first encouragement.

Charlie had his stopwatch in hand. As she and Wonder came off the far turn, Ashleigh prepared herself for the gallop. She saw Charlie lower his hand, and immediately she dropped into a crouch over the filly's withers, giving Wonder rein.

Wonder exploded forward, stretching her legs and lengthening her stride. Her mane whipped back into

Ashleigh's face. White railing posts flashed by Ashleigh's eyes in a blur. The sounds of Wonder's pounding hoofbeats and steady, snorted breaths echoed in her ears.

Ashleigh held the filly in a collected gallop as they flew along the inside rail, off the turn, into the backstretch. Charlie's instructions were to gallop Wonder for the first half mile, then breeze her flat out through another half mile. Ashleigh watched the marking poles, ready to further ease her hold on the reins and let the filly all the way out.

At the half-mile pole, Ashleigh dropped lower in her crouch, kneaded her hands along Wonder's neck, and cried, "Go!" Wonder instantly changed gears, lengthening her stride, and increasing her already rapid pace. They were flying; the filly was performing at her peak. Ashleigh didn't need a stopwatch to know Wonder was covering the ground in impressive time and doing it easily. A half-mile breeze was nothing to her.

They pounded off the far turn and down the stretch. As they streaked past Charlie in a copper blur, Ashleigh drew back on the reins and stood up in the stirrups. Wonder obediently dropped down from a gallop to a canter.

"That's my girl!" Ashleigh praised, firmly patting Wonder's arched neck. "Good job. Charlie ought to be happy with that!"

Wonder's steps were full of spring as Ashleigh turned her and headed her back toward the entrance gap. There was barely any sweat on her copper coat. The workout hadn't taken much out of the filly at all.

Charlie strode toward them as Ashleigh rode off the oval. The old trainer wasn't one to show his feelings, but Ashleigh saw the twinkle in his blue eyes. She noticed the other trainers and riders were watching them intently, too.

"Not bad," Charlie said.

Ashleigh grinned down at him. "And what does that mean? What was our time?"

"She galloped the mile in one-thirty-nine, and did the last half in a shade under forty-six—just about where I wanted her to work. How did she feel?"

"Great, and she was listening. I didn't have any trouble with her." Ashleigh threw her leg over the saddle and jumped to the ground. As she did, Wonder butted her head forward to catch Charlie firmly and affectionately in the shoulder.

"You know you did okay, don't ya, little lady?" Charlie rubbed Wonder's velvet nose. "Just don't get too cocky. You'll have your work cut out for you this weekend."

Ashleigh removed her helmet, and her dark hair cascaded down to her shoulders. She shook it from her eyes. At fifteen, she was five foot three, slim and athletic. That's the way she needed to be if she was going to fulfill her dream of being a jockey.

"Okay," Charlie said after he'd checked the filly over, "get her cooled out and in her stall. I'm going to hang around here and watch a couple of workouts." He shuffled back to the rail, and Ashleigh led Wonder toward the huge, immaculate barn complex and tree-shaded stable yard. She waved and answered the greetings of the grooms leading horses to and from the stables, then untacked the filly and took her for a walk under the trees.

Jilly Gordon joined Ashleigh as she was finishing Wonder's walk. Petite, fair-haired, and twenty-three, Jilly was Wonder's jockey and rode some of the other Townsend Acres horses as well. "Nice workout," Jilly beamed. "Hope she does that well for me at Pimlico, for the Preakness."

"You know she will," Ashleigh said with a laugh. Which was true. Jilly had exactly the right touch for the filly—a light hand and gentle manner. She used her voice to get results, not heavy handling.

"Things are definitely heating up," Jilly said. "Everyone's talking a match race. The mood's sure changed from a year ago."

"It sure has," Ashleigh sniffed. "Nobody thought much of Wonder then, did they?" She led Wonder into her stall and unclipped her lead shank. Wonder went straight to her hay net to tear off a mouthful of hay. Ashleigh stepped back outside and fastened the stall shut just as Charlie and Hank, one of the oldest grooms at the farm, were walking up the aisle.

"She knocked the wind out of 'em—and they deserve it," Hank was saying to Charlie. "I always said this filly was going to be good."

"I wouldn't count out the rest of the competition just yet," Charlie said shortly. "I just watched Townsend Prince's workout. The colt's not going to make it easy for us in the Preakness, and that West Coast colt, Mercy Man, is training real well, I hear. No one's going to walk all over the field, our filly included."

"You're too pessimistic, Charlie," Jilly called as the two men reached the stall.

"Better than being too confident," he shot back.

"The Prince looked good?" Ashleigh asked as she hung Wonder's lead shank on a hook outside the stall.

"They only breezed him three furlongs, then galloped him out, but I couldn't see anything to find fault with. He was moving real smooth."

"Too bad," Ashleigh said. But Townsend Prince had gone into the Derby looking like a winner—and had lost to Wonder.

"The van's set to leave here about six tomorrow morning," Charlie said. "You riding up in the van with me, Jilly?"

"Yup. I don't know if my old pickup would make it all the way to Maryland and back."

"Time you bought a new one," Hank said, "with all these purses you've been winning. I hear some other trainers have been talking to you about riding for them. I don't imagine Townsend and Maddock will like that too much." He gave her a sly grin.

Jilly tossed her long blond braid over her shoulder. "You've got big ears, Hank. Who I ride for is my business, but right now riding Wonder's my number-one priority."

"That ought to keep you fairly busy." Hank chuckled. "Townsend's already talking of running her in the Breeder's Cup in the fall, and you got a good many races between now and then, eh, Charlie?"

Charlie grunted. "Right now I'm concentrating on the race this coming weekend."

Ashleigh glanced at her watch. "I'd better get going or I'll miss the bus!" She threw Wonder a kiss and gave the others a wave, then hurried out of the stable building and down the long drive leading to the breeding barns and her family's house opposite them. As usual, she sighed with pleasure at the view from the drive. Green paddocks spread out over the rolling hills to either side, and sleek Thoroughbreds grazed on the thick Kentucky bluegrass. In several paddocks, young foals scampered playfully beside their dams.

The mares and foals were Ashleigh's parents' responsibility as breeding managers of the farm.

Ashleigh jogged up the porch steps of the house and through the front door. She heard voices in the kitchen. "Rory, get your nose out of that horse magazine and go get dressed!"

Ashleigh stuck her head around the kitchen doorway as her eighteen-year-old sister, Caroline, pulled a magazine away from their ten-year-old brother and shooed him out of his chair.

"Caro, you're a pain!" Rory cried. "I was almost finished."

"You have to catch the bus. Justin's going to pick me up in a minute, and I haven't even finished my hair." Caro looked over and saw Ashleigh. "How's Ashleigh's Wonder?" she asked teasingly.

Ashleigh smiled at Caro using Wonder's "official" name. Three years earlier, Ashleigh's determined nursing had saved Wonder's life. When Bill, one of the grooms, had suggested naming the newborn filly Ashleigh's Wonder, everyone had agreed and the name had stuck.

"Great—she's all set to go to Pimlico."

"Brad worked the Prince, I suppose," Caro said.

"Charlie said the colt looked good."

"I just hope you beat him again this weekend—give him something to worry about," Caroline said firmly. She had plenty of reason to gloat over Brad's defeat in the Derby. Brad and Caroline had dated until the previous fall, when he'd suddenly dropped her for another girl. He'd been a complete jerk about it, and it had taken Caro a long time to get over the hurt.

"You'll win," Rory called from the doorway.

"Will you get going!" Caroline cried. "If you miss the bus, you know what Mom and Dad will have to say."

Rory wrinkled his nose and shot off up the stairs.

"I've got to change, too," Ashleigh said. She grabbed an apple from the bowl on the table for breakfast. Fifteen minutes later she ran out of the house and jogged down the long drive to the main road, reaching the stop just as the bus was approaching. She bounded up the steps and saw the curly blond head of her best friend, Linda March, halfway down the aisle. She slid into the next seat.

"So," Linda asked expectantly, "how did it go this morning?" Linda's father was a trainer, and she was as avid a horse lover as Ashleigh.

"Great!" Ashleigh said. "All set." The two of them talked nonstop about the race during the ride into Lexington. When the bus dropped them in front of the doors of Henry Clay Middle School, they gathered their books and hurried into the building. As they stepped inside, Ashleigh stopped dead in her tracks and stared at the banner strung across the hall. GOOD LUCK, WONDER AND ASHLEIGH! it read.

A cheer went up from the dozens of kids in the hall.

Ashleigh was flabbergasted. She swung toward Linda. "Did you know about this?"

Linda gave her a silly grin. Ashleigh saw some of her other friends, Corey Jacobs, Jennifer Marshall, and Stacy DeScala. They were all smiling.

"What do you think?" Corey hurried over, bubbly and outgoing as usual. "Do you like it?"

For a second Ashleigh could only gape. It amazed her to see everyone standing there, cheering for her and Wonder. She'd always been too busy training Wonder to get very involved with all the extra stuff at school.

"Well, say *something*." Jennifer laughed. With her honey-blond hair and perfect figure, she was definitely the most popular girl in ninth grade, at least with the boys.

Ashleigh felt her cheeks flushing. This was unreal. But finally she grinned. "It's great! Thanks . . . thanks a lot!"

"We'll all be watching the race on TV," Corey said brightly. "And I mean everybody. I'm having a Preakness party that afternoon, and I've invited the whole class!"

"You have?" Ashleigh gulped, wishing Corey wasn't quite so enthusiastic. She and Wonder would have a lot to live up to!

The phone rang on Thursday night as Ashleigh was hurriedly packing for the family's trip to Maryland the next morning. Caroline answered the extension in their shared bedroom.

"Hello?" She gave Ashleigh a devilish grin and handed over the phone. "Guess who?"

From her sister's expression, Ashleigh had a pretty good idea that the caller was Mike Reese. Ashleigh had met Mike that winter at a basketball game and had hit it off with him instantly when she'd discovered he was training his own horses. Mike also happened to be a blondly handsome and very popular junior.

Ashleigh grabbed the phone from her sister's hand. "Hello," she said.

"Hi, Ashleigh. I just wanted to call to wish you luck. You must be feeling pretty excited."

"I really am," Ashleigh agreed, turning her back on her sister's grinning face. "I think I feel more nervous than I did before the Derby."

"Wonder has more to live up to now. But she can do it." Ashleigh could hear the smile in Mike's voice. "You're leaving in the morning?"

"First thing."

"I'll be watching the race and cheering her on. I'll give you a call when you get back, okay?"

"Sure, I'd like that. And thanks a lot for calling."

"See you in the winner's circle."

11

Ashleigh smiled, remembering the last time Mike had said that—she and Wonder *had* ended up in the winner's circle. As she hung up the phone, she hoped his words were a good omen.

2

THE WINDSHIELD WIPERS WERE BEATING RAPIDLY AS MR. GRIF-fen maneuvered the family station wagon down the interstate into Baltimore. "I hope this lets up before tomorrow," he said.

Mrs. Griffen checked the map in her hands. "Let's not worry about it now. Let's just get to the track in one piece. I hope you can see where you're going better than I can."

"How much longer?" Rory groaned from the back-seat.

"Not much," his father answered. "And no complaining. I've got enough to think about."

Ashleigh turned to her brother. "You can come to the stable with me when we get to the track, okay?"

Rory looked a little more cheerful. "You think all this rain will hurt Wonder's chances?" he asked.

"It's not her favorite surface." Ashleigh was trying

to stay optimistic, but it wasn't easy. A muddy track would make the race much harder on Wonder and could seriously affect her performance.

For the rest of the trip, the family was silent. Half an hour later, they saw the signs directing them to Pimlico. The rain had let up a little—it wasn't coming down in sheets, but it was steady. Mrs. Griffen turned and looked into the backseat. "Ashleigh, we'll drop you and Rory on the backside while we get the motel sorted out. We'll meet you back here in about an hour."

Mr. Griffen pulled into the backside lot and parked near the barns. Ashleigh and Rory climbed out and waved their parents off. "Stay right with me, Rory," Ashleigh ordered, "or I'll have a heck of a time finding you." She set off determinedly, already knowing her way around. She'd spent a lot of hours on the Pimlico backside when Wonder had raced there the previous summer.

A few people were gathered in the protection of the barns, but it was a quiet time of the day, close to dinner, when the stable hands had some hours to themselves.

Charlie and Jilly were standing near Wonder's stall talking to Ken Maddock. Jilly waved. "You guys must have had a rough trip."

"It wasn't great," Ashleigh agreed.

"Weather's sure not on our side," Charlie grumbled. "The filly's fine," he added. "The trip didn't bother her. She's settled right in. Better go say hello to her."

Wonder was nickering impatiently, waiting for Ashleigh. With a grin, Ashleigh strode over to the stall, took Wonder's head in her hands, and gave her a kiss. "Yeah, I'm glad to see you, too."

"The track's real slop," Maddock said to Charlie. "I just went out and had a look. I don't see it drying out completely unless we get a real sunny, breezy day tomorrow."

"That's what I was thinking." Charlie rubbed his chin thoughtfully. "There's a few mudders in the race. What do you think of that long shot, Wanderkill?"

"He won in the mud down in Florida, though he doesn't do much on a fast track. Strawberry Fields could be a colt to worry about if the track is off—so Bennet, his trainer, is telling everyone. Neither of them has any class, though. I can't see them pulling any big surprises tomorrow, even if the track stays sloppy."

"An off track ought to help you," Charlie said. "This track has a reputation for favoring front-running speed horses when it's fast."

"An off track, not slop," Maddock said. "Well, I'm

supposed to be meeting the Townsends for dinner and that pre-race party. See you all later."

As he walked away down the long, horse-crammed barn, Jilly frowned. "The Townsends never take you to dinner, Charlie. You think they would have tonight at least."

"Wouldn't want to go if they asked me," Charlie said. "All that social hobnobbing's not my style. I'd rather be here with the horses."

Ashleigh laughed. She could picture the Townsends with their wealthy, horse-owning friends, all of them expensively dressed and probably sipping champagne. No, it wasn't Charlie's scene at all.

Rory walked over to Charlie with an eager face. "I can help you if you want, Charlie—at least until my parents come back."

Charlie scratched his gray head. "Nothing much to do, really. The filly's all settled. I was just going to stroll around and check out some of the other horses in the field. I suppose you could come along."

"All right," Rory agreed happily. As the old man and the boy moved off, Rory's voice echoed back, "Can we take a look at Mercy Man? What do you think of Sandia . . . and that other horse . . ."

Jilly winked at Ashleigh. "Sounds like Charlie's got a budding trainer on his hands. Charlie would never admit it, but he's got a soft spot for kids."

Ashleigh agreed, remembering her own experiences with the old trainer. "But I was scared to death of him at first."

"So was I, but I think he's lightened up a little since he's training again and doesn't feel useless."

"Was the track sloppy when you worked Wonder this morning?" Ashleigh asked.

"No, it was fast. It didn't start raining until late morning. We only gave her a light gallop. She felt great and was really taking to the surface." Jilly frowned. "That's why this rain bothers me. Charlie's right about an off track favoring late closers like Townsend Prince. But, who knows." Jilly crossed her fingers hopefully. "Maybe the sun will be out tomorrow, and we won't have anything to worry about!"

The skies were still leaden gray in the morning. The rain had been replaced by a heavy mist, and the air was damp and raw. Since the Griffens had been exhausted by the long trip, they'd all slept late, and it was already close to nine when Ashleigh's parents dropped her off at the track. They were taking Rory with them to see the sights of Baltimore. He protested fiercely, but Mrs. Griffen was firm. "Ashleigh will have enough to do without having to keep an eye on you. Don't worry, we'll get back here long before the race goes off."

The backside was a hive of activity compared to the

17

night before. Grooms led sheeted horses over the drier gravel paths, and the reporters were in full swing, with camera crews making preparations for the live coverage of the race. The few horses that had been worked on the track early that morning were already cleaned up and back in their stalls.

Ashleigh found Charlie near the end of the barn, talking to some of the grooms. Wonder looked alert and happy. The weather didn't seem to be affecting her spirits, and she nickered as Ashleigh came up to the stall. Charlie or Terry Bush had covered the filly with a light sheet to keep out the dampness and chill, and Wonder's hay net and water bucket were full. Ashleigh went into the stall and looked the filly over carefully anyway.

"Jilly and I are going out to have a firsthand look at the track," Charlie called from outside the stall. "Why don't you come along? Terry's just down the barn. He'll keep an eye on the filly."

"Sure," Ashleigh said, anxious to see the track herself. She'd worked the filly in the mud plenty of times and knew it was a very messy experience. She didn't envy Jilly.

The grandstand was still empty, except for the crews making preparations for the crowds that would soon start filtering in. Several tents were set up in the infield, although the weather would probably keep some spectators away.

The three of them walked up along the outside rail of the track, not far from where the starting gate would be positioned. The track crew was busy all around the dirt oval, trying to speed the drying of the surface. They had a long way to go to make up for the previous day's downpour.

Charlie shook his head, and droplets of water dripped off the brim of his felt hat. "If this mist lets up, we'll be lucky if it's upgraded to fair by the time of the race. And we'll have the fields in the seven races ahead of us churning it up real good. Looks like real heavy going along the inside," he said to Jilly. "We'll have to keep a close eye on how the earlier races play out—see if the inside horses look like they're struggling."

Jilly nodded, intent on Charlie's words. "At least she's pulled the five-post position and won't have to break on the rail."

None of them had noticed Brad Townsend walk up. He was in jeans and an expensive slicker, and his dark hair was curling slightly in the mist. He nodded to them as he passed, but didn't smile. He didn't look too happy either.

"Well, no point in getting ourselves depressed out here," Charlie said. "Might not hurt to take the filly for a little walk around the yard, missy," he said to Ashleigh. "Keep her limber and keep this damp from setting in." He strode off with the girls following.

"He looks worried," Ashleigh whispered to Jilly.

"I don't know. It's hard to tell with Charlie. He could be scheming, too."

An hour before post time, Ashleigh finished giving Wonder a meticulous grooming, which probably would all go to waste before Wonder got out to the saddling area. The mist had continued, and the track hadn't improved much since morning. Still, the filly looked elegant and knew it, too. As Charlie prepared to lead Wonder to the receiving barn, Ashleigh glanced down the aisle and saw the crowd outside Townsend Prince's stall. Of course, there had been plenty of media people around Wonder's stall, too, but Charlie had herded them off. He didn't like too much excitement around the stall just before a race. Mr. Townsend was dressed in a suit and tie under a light raincoat and looked every bit the owner of one of the largest and most successful Thoroughbred farms in Kentucky. Ashleigh saw that Brad had also changed into a sports jacket under his raincoat. Beside him stood his girlfriend, Melinda Westwood. Her hair was perfectly cut, and her silk suit was obviously expensive. She looked as if she belonged in the Townsend's wealthy set. Ashleigh unconsciously glanced down at her own jeans and jacket. There was a reason, of course, for Brad and Melinda to be dressed. If either the Prince or Wonder won, Brad would go to the winner's circle with his father to collect the trophy. If Ashleigh went into the winner's circle, it would be as Wonder's groom.

An hour later, all of them damp from the persistent mist, Charlie gave Jilly a leg into the saddle. "Like I said," he told her, "try to get her right up near the lead, but stay off the rail. From the way the last races have been running, that inside lane's real soft. It'd be too tiring on her. You'll just have to take the chance of some horse closing on your inside. Keep your eyes open, and just let her run the best race she can."

Jilly nodded, fastened her chin strap, and gathered the reins. Ashleigh dropped a kiss on the filly's nose. "Do your best, girl." She looked up to Jilly and gave her a smile. "Good luck."

"Thanks."

As the field moved out onto the track, Ashleigh and Charlie made their way through a sea of umbrellas into the grandstand to the box seats Mr. Townsend had reserved for the Griffens and Charlie. The Townsends were in another box with some of their friends.

Ashleigh looked across to the odds board. Townsend Prince and Wonder were the cofavorites. Mercy Man was the third betting choice, but because of the sloppy track, Strawberry Fields and Wanderkill were also being heavily bet.

"She looked good in the walking ring, Ash," her mother said encouragingly.

Ashleigh smiled, but she felt tense.

"Let's just hope the track doesn't put her off," Charlie said.

The field had finished their warm-up jog and were approaching the gate. This was always the worst time for Ashleigh—the anxious moments of anticipation waiting for the race to go off. Fortunately the horses loaded smoothly. Ashleigh gripped the binoculars her father had handed her, though she wouldn't need them until the field was in the backstretch. The gates flew open. "They're off!" the announcer cried.

Wonder broke sharply, bursting from the middle of the pack. As they'd expected, Sandia, a front-running speed horse, took the early lead on the inside, but his jockey was holding him off the rail. Gyro moved up beside him, and Jilly angled Wonder across the track to settle just behind the two leaders.

"Good," Charlie said. "Just where we want her."

The pace was slow as the field swept around the clubhouse turn—evidence of the sloppy surface—and the first quarter went in a moderate twenty-six seconds. Ashleigh knew the slow pace would help them; Wonder wouldn't use up her strength too soon. She raised her glasses to her eyes and glued them to Wonder as the field moved into the backstretch. Sandia and Gyro were already struggling to hold the lead.

Wonder was slowly moving up on their outside, but Jilly was still reserving her—she hadn't let the filly all the way out. Ashleigh swept her glasses over the rest of the field. Townsend Prince and Mercy Man were in sixth and seventh, and neither colt seemed happy with the surface. But Strawberry Fields and Wanderkill were running happily through the slop! Ashleigh groaned as she saw the two mudders moving up through the field.

"Don't start worrying yet," Charlie told her.

"The half in forty-seven and three," the track announcer called. "Sandia's holding on to the lead, but the colt's tiring. Gyro's dropped out of it. Ashleigh's Wonder, still under a hold, is moving up outside of Sandia. Strawberry Fields is gaining quickly on the outside, now into fourth, with Wanderkill moving between horses and looking for an opening inside. Townsend Prince and Mercy Man have yet to make their moves. Townsend Prince in sixth, Mercy Man dropping back to eighth. The track's not to his liking."

The field was moving into the far turn. Ashleigh watched intently, waiting for the late runners to click into gear. Sandia was fading. Without effort Wonder swept past him to a length lead, but it was too early yet to cheer. Townsend Prince hadn't made his run yet. Then Ashleigh saw what she'd been dreading.

"And here comes Townsend Prince!" the announcer cried. "Roaring up on the outside! Ashleigh's Wonder has the lead by a length and is digging in, but Strawberry Fields and Wanderkill are in full gear, too! Strawberry Fields in second. Wanderkill in third and looking for running room. But Townsend Prince is breezing right by them! And *down* the stretch they come!

"Ashleigh's Wonder holding on to the lead—Townsend Prince coming on to challenge! It's going to be a battle to the wire—the race everyone was looking for! A sixteenth of a mile to go, but here comes Wanderkill, making a run on the inside! Vargos is trying to squeeze him through on the rail!"

The announcer was going hoarse. Ashleigh was gripping the binoculars so tightly, her knuckles were white. "Hold on, Wonder!" she cried. "You can do it!"

"Three of them heading down to the wire!" the announcer shouted. "Ashleigh's Wonder holding on by a neck. Wanderkill still trying to squeeze through on the rail."

Ashleigh gasped as she saw Wanderkill slip into the slot Jilly had left open on the rail. But there wasn't enough room, and the colt swerved out, right into Wonder!

"Ashleigh's Wonder's been bumped and is forced to steady," the announcer shouted. "And Townsend

24

Prince has taken the lead! Wanderkill surges through on the rail into second. Ashleigh's Wonder is between them a half-length behind after being steadied. But the filly's coming back, pushing between the leaders. Will she have time? No! They're under the wire. Townsend Prince, Wanderkill, Ashleigh's Wonder, heads apart! Then Strawberry Fields a half-length farther back, and Mercy Man, settling for fifth . . ."

Charlie had pulled off his hat and was angrily slamming his fist into it. "Jilly better protest. Vargos lost us the race!"

No sooner were the words out of his mouth, than the announcer returned. "A spectacular finish, but the inquiry sign is up. There's no question the filly was badly bumped in the stretch. The results are unofficial."

"Let's go!" Charlie said, already starting down the stairs. Ashleigh was right behind him. By the time they reached the track, Jilly had pulled Wonder up near the gap to the backside and was talking with an official. With the exception of Townsend Prince, who was being ridden to the winner's circle, the other horses were coming off the track.

Jilly and Wonder were coated with mud, and Jilly was furious. "I lodged a protest," she said as soon as Charlie and Ashleigh reached her side. "Vargos's horse swerved right into us, nearly knocked Wonder off her feet. She could have held on to win if she hadn't been bumped! There wasn't room inside us. He shouldn't have tried it!"

"When you're going for the big time, you take chances," Charlie said. "But you did right. There's no way the protest won't stand."

Ashleigh had gone to Wonder. The filly was breathing hard, obviously upset by the interference during the race, but she immediately dropped her head and nuzzled Ashleigh's hand.

"You did a good job, girl—a fantastic job! It's not your fault you didn't win." Ashleigh turned to Jilly, who'd dismounted and was removing Wonder's saddle. "She had something left?"

"Yes, she did! The track was taking more out of her than usual, but she wasn't finished." Jilly pulled off the saddle, and Terry hurried up to throw a sheet over Wonder's muddy, steaming back.

Just then the official who was standing with them put his ear to his hand-held communicator, then nodded to Charlie with a smile. "Upheld," he said.

The odds board flashed the final results. Wonder was put up into second. Wanderkill was taken down to third for interference.

"A little consolation anyway," Charlie said. "Let's get this filly cooled out and cleaned up."

But Townsend Prince had still won it, Ashleigh thought, and Brad wasn't going to let her forget it.

3

THE GRIFFENS ARRIVED BACK AT TOWNSEND ACRES LATE SUN-
day night. They were all exhausted, especially Ashleigh, but Caro was curled up on her bed, ready to
talk as Ashleigh changed into her pajamas. "She
should have won it! Everyone I talked to said the
same thing. Mike especially. He and Chad watched
the race at Justin's." Chad McGowan was Mike's best
friend, and Justin's younger brother. "And the way
Brad was gloating in the winner's circle . . . it was
so disgusting!" Caro continued.

"I didn't see him." Ashleigh pulled her sweatshirt
over her head. "I was on the backside with Wonder."

"Well, you can imagine it."

"Mmmm, I heard him bragging to some of the reporters back at the barn. But like Charlie says, it
doesn't mean anything." Ashleigh stifled a yawn.
"It's only talk."

"The papers had some good things to say about Wonder anyway," Caro went on. "But they're really talking about the Belmont being a match race now." Suddenly Caro jumped off her bed and ran to the closet. "And wait till you see what I got this weekend! Marcy and I went shopping, and I finally found a dress for the prom." She whipped it out and held it in front of her for Ashleigh to see. The satin gown was long and in a shade of blue that almost perfectly matched Caroline's eyes.

"Wow, it's great—really pretty," Ashleigh exclaimed, for a moment forgetting her tiredness. "God, I can't believe you're graduating already. It's going to be strange not having you here next fall."

"I'll be home on weekends," Caroline said cheerfully. "And Justin will have his car at the campus, so we can drive back from Louisville on Friday nights."

Ashleigh yawned again. "I've got to go to bed, Caro. I can't keep my eyes open. We can talk more tomorrow." Ashleigh threw back her covers and crawled under them. Her bed had never felt so good. "See you in the morning." She plumped up her pillow and nestled her head.

"Oh," Caro said. "I almost forgot to tell you! Mike called tonight. He said he'd talk to you sometime tomorrow."

"Did he?" Ashleigh smiled, and with a contented sigh, she closed her eyes.

"You got cheated!" Corey cried as Ashleigh and Linda walked into school the next morning. "She should have won! Aren't you angry?"

"A little," Ashleigh admitted. "But like Charlie says, you win some, you lose some."

"Sure, if it's a fair loss."

"Wonder still ran a darned good race," Linda said.

"True." Corey frowned, then shrugged her shoulders. "You'll beat him next time. Listen, before I forget to ask, I need some help on the graduation committee—you know, for setup and stuff. We've got less than a month. You guys want to volunteer? It'll only be a couple of afternoons—"

Wonder wouldn't arrive back from Pimlico for a couple of days, but Ashleigh went up to the stable yard anyway that afternoon. As she arrived, Mike drove into the yard in his small pickup. He waved and gave her a big smile. "Hi, there," he called. Ashleigh waved back and waited as he walked over. "Missed you last night," he said.

"We got home pretty late."

"Sorry about the way the race played out, but she did a great job. You'll get him next time. How'd she come out of it?"

"Not bad, considering. She was pretty tired, but she ate, which is a good sign."

29

"It was pretty amazing watching her come back like she did. She's a fighter."

Ashleigh smiled. "She sure is. How's Jazzman coming along?"

"Good. I'm thinking of starting him at Churchill Downs the end of June. Our other colt needs to mature a little more. We probably won't start him until the end of summer. Listen, why don't you come over to Whitebrook one afternoon and have a look? I'd like to show you our setup. I could drive you over after school."

Ashleigh hesitated, caught by surprise. But it took her only a second to make up her mind. She'd been wanting to see Mike's farm. Charlie had been there and had told her that Mike and Chad were doing an impressive job. "Thanks," she said. "I'd like to, and this week won't be that busy, since we're giving Wonder a week off."

"How about Wednesday? That okay?"

"Sure."

They talked a few minutes longer, then Mike headed back to his truck. "See you Wednesday," he called.

Ashleigh smiled and waved him off, but as she led Wonder toward the barn, Brad Townsend stepped out of the shadows. "So you're giving your boyfriend free tours of the farm again," he jeered.

"He's just a friend who came by to say hello."

Brad lazily stuffed his hands into the pockets of his jeans and studied her. "I suppose he and his father need all the help they can get. That place of theirs isn't much. I hear his father used to train a second-rate string of horses in Florida."

With an effort Ashleigh stopped herself from snapping back. She'd learned the hard way that you didn't tell off Brad Townsend. She started forward into the barn.

"Your filly came out of the Preakness pretty used up," Brad called after her. "She'll need a lot of luck if she's going to go the Belmont distance."

"She had a rough trip!"

"Think what you like. I'd say this next race may just be too much for her."

"You so sure the Prince is going to like the extra distance?" Ashleigh shot back.

"He'll eat it up," Brad answered confidently. With that Brad sauntered off, but Ashleigh'd seen his self-confident smile waver for an instant. He wasn't as sure of the outcome as he pretended to be.

Wednesday, Mike picked her up outside school as he'd promised. Since he was two years older, he went to the same high school that Caroline did, which was right across the huge green. It was an absolutely perfect day, sunny and warm. As they drove through the landscape of tree-lined pastures toward Versailles, a spring-scented breeze blew in through the open windows of his pickup, ruffling Ashleigh's hair. They talked easily for the rest of the drive through the rolling horse country. Mike pulled off between a set of white-painted gate posts and drove down a graveled drive. Ashleigh could see the house and barns in the distance. Whitebrook Farm was modest compared to the lavish spread of Townsend Acres, but it was efficiently laid out.

"The house and the main barn are part of the original farm," Mike told her. "Nearly two hundred years old. We added that one stable building and upgraded the training track."

"It's nice," Ashleigh said as Mike parked by the stable. He led the way around the main barn and paused by one of the paddock railings. He pointed to two young horses scampering across the grass.

"Those are our yearlings. We bought one at the Keeneland Auction. The gray was bred here—first crop of our single stallion." He laughed. "It's going to take a while to build things up, but come on and see Jazzman and Indigo."

They went into the newer stable building. An old groom waved to them from the end of the aisle. "Hi, Len," Mike called. "Can you get me Jazzman's tack? I'm going to work him for a while." Len nodded and disappeared into the tack room.

Mike paused by the stall of a dark gray colt. "This

is Indigo. Chad's doing most of the work with him. He's still got some growing up to do, but I think he's going to turn into a good racehorse." Ashleigh admired the rangy animal, who came over to the stall door to inspect his visitors. The colt had beautiful confirmation, but she could see he hadn't grown into himself yet.

"And down here," Mike added with a glimmer of pride, "is Jazzman." The horse already had his coal black head over the door and was whickering to Mike. "Hiya, fella." Mike grinned. "Ready to go out?" Mike unlatched the stall, clipped a lead shank to the colt's halter, and led him out. He glanced at Ashleigh expectantly. "What do you think?"

Ashleigh was still studying the gleaming black horse. The colt had wonderfully sleek lines, powerful muscles, a deep chest, and perfect legs and feet. "He's a beauty! How did you manage to get him cheap at auction?"

"He was on the small side as a yearling—he's grown like a shot in the last year—and he doesn't have Wonder's bloodlines. Not that his background's bad. I decided not to work him until this afternoon," Mike said. "Actually, I wanted to show him off, and I thought maybe you'd like to try him out yourself."

Ashleigh turned to him in surprise. "Really? I'd love it, if you don't mind."

"I don't mind, and I know you can handle him.

He's a real gentleman as long as he knows he can't get the better of you."

The groom returned holding a saddle and bridle, and Mike made introductions. "Len, this is a friend of mine, Ashleigh Griffen, as in Ashleigh's Wonder."

Len's face immediately creased in a smile. "Glad to meet you. Some filly you got there."

"Len was with my father training down in Florida before we bought Whitebrook a few years ago. He's been in the business for years."

"Do you know Charlie Burke?" Ashleigh asked.

"Known Charlie longer than either of us probably care to remember. We had a nice chat the day he came over with Mike. Glad he's got a good horse to train again. He's got too much talent to waste in retirement."

"He seems a lot happier now." Ashleigh smiled.

"With good reason. The Townsends were crazy to put him out to pasture, but I guess they've seen the error of their ways, with the filly doing so well."

Mike had finished tacking up Jazzman. "I thought I'd let Ashleigh try him," he said to Len. "After I get him warmed up. Come out and watch."

"Wouldn't miss it." Len followed them as they left the stable. Mike mounted the high-spirited colt, and the two moved out onto the oval.

"I think he's got a good one here," Len said to Ashleigh. "And I've seen a lot of horses. The boy deserves it. He and his dad have worked plenty hard."

They lapsed into silence as Mike moved Jazzman from a jog to a slow gallop. The colt moved beautifully, and Mike rode with relaxed skill. He kept the colt in perfect control without ever hard-handling him. Ashleigh couldn't help comparing Mike's riding style to Brad's. Mike was just as good, or better, but he wasn't trying to tell the world how great he was. Horse and rider lapped the track several times, then drew up near the outside rail.

"Want to try him?" he said to Ashleigh. "Just watch him on the turns. He's still a little green and may try to pull out."

Ashleigh was wearing her good jeans and sneakers, not boots, but she wasn't about to pass up the chance. She nodded and grinned as she ducked under the rail. Mike dismounted, handed her his hard hat to wear, then gave her a leg into the saddle. She settled herself, speaking quietly to the colt and patting his neck. When Mike stepped back, she urged Jazzman up the track at a jog, until she felt comfortable with the colt's particular habits and style. Then she gave him the signal to gallop. He jumped out like the eager young horse he was. Ashleigh steadied him slightly and held him in near the rail. When the colt started to pull out at the turn, as Mike had warned, Ashleigh held him on course with firm pressure on her inside rein.

She could feel the difference between this colt and Wonder. Jazzman was still green and a little awkward. But while Wonder would have been impatiently trying to get her head right from the start, Jazzman was content to relax and lay off a hard pace. Mike had told Ashleigh that he thought the colt was a closer, and she figured he was right.

Ashleigh was beaming when she pulled the colt up beside Mike and Len. "You've got something here."

Mike tried to hide his own reaction, but Ashleigh could see how proud he was. She was amazed that he had trained the colt by himself. No wonder Charlie was impressed.

The rest of the afternoon flew by. Before Ashleigh knew it, it was five o'clock and time to go home. Mike dropped her by her front door. "I'll stop by later in the week," he told her. "Okay?"

"Sure, and thanks, Mike. I had a great time!" Ashleigh's eyes met Mike's and they smiled at each other. Then Ashleigh looked away, suddenly feeling awkward.

"Well, thanks again," she said again, lamely. Her cheeks were burning, but her heart was happy as she walked slowly into the house.

4

ASHLEIGH STARED THROUGH THE TINY WINDOW AS THE PLANE circled in its approach to LaGuardia Airport. Beyond, she saw the skyline of Manhattan, the blue waters of converging rivers and ocean, buildings and streets all laid out in miniature. It had been a week since Mr. Townsend had stopped by the Griffenses' to tell Ashleigh and her parents that he'd arranged round-trip airfare for Ashleigh to fly to New York for the Belmont. Ashleigh still couldn't believe it! And now she was actually here.

She settled back in her seat as the plane made a smooth landing and taxied to the gate. She mentally ran through the instructions she'd been given: Go straight to the baggage claim area. Someone would meet her there and drive her to Belmont, where she'd stay in a motel room with Jilly. Ashleigh smiled, remembering how worried her mother had been about

37

Ashleigh arriving in New York alone. "Don't talk to any strangers," she'd warned. "Stay in lighted areas, and don't leave your luggage." Mr. Griffen had finally intervened with a laugh. "Stop! She'll be fine, and someone from the farm *is* meeting her."

The other passengers had risen, ready to push out into the aisle. Ashleigh unfastened her seat belt, picked up the shoulder bag her sister had lent her, and stood up. Gradually, she edged off the plane with the others, through the covered passage and into the terminal. The easiest thing was just to follow the crowd, but she saw signs, too, pointing to the baggage area.

There were so many people! And everyone seemed to be in a hurry. She was bumped and shoved, and few people said "Excuse me." But she managed to follow the arrows, and eventually she reached the baggage area and saw her flight number on the sign above one of the baggage carousels. She glanced around at all the strange faces, wondering who would be meeting her and how she'd ever spot them.

Then she saw a waving hand and a familiar, smiling face. Jilly pushed through the crowd toward her.

"Found you!" Jilly cried. "Have a good trip?" she added as the two girls hugged.

"Incredible, but I'm sure glad to see you! How'd you get here? Did someone lend you a car?"

"No, madam," Jilly said haughtily. "*We* have a

limo waiting for us, compliments of Mr. Townsend. I came over with the driver."

"A limo, huh?" Ashleigh laughed. "We're in the big time."

"And I could get used to it real easy! Let's get your luggage and get out of here." Like the experienced traveler she'd become in the last year, Jilly drew Ashleigh through the crowd to the edge of the carousel. She grabbed Ashleigh's one piece of luggage as it came around, and a moment later they were wiggling back through the crowd to the exit doors.

A wave of warm air engulfed them as they stepped outside. It reeked of exhaust and diesel fumes from the many waiting taxis and buses. Horns tooted impatiently, and brakes squealed from sudden stops. "The limo's right up here," Jilly said.

With Ashleigh gazing eagerly around, they strode up the sidewalk to the gleaming black stretch limo parked at the curb. The uniformed driver was standing beside the open rear door. He nodded at them and quickly took Ashleigh's suitcase. "Thanks," she said, as she slid into the plushly upholstered rear seat. She lifted her eyebrows at Jilly and whispered, "Nice. If the guys back home could see us now."

"I've been thinking the same thing."

Within seconds the driver was behind the wheel and had the limo moving smoothly and silently out into traffic.

"I've never seen so much traffic," Ashleigh said as they left the airport and edged onto an expressway.

"You're in New York, don't forget, and it's Friday."

Ashleigh turned back to Jilly. She was feeling a little dazed, but incredibly excited. "How's Wonder?"

"Fine. She shipped well and really seems to like the track up here. We put in some nice workouts this week."

"And Charlie?"

"He doesn't say so, but I think he's having a ball. He keeps running into people he hasn't seen in years, and they start talking about old times. And this track is incredible," Jilly added. "One of the other jockeys was telling me they have over two thousand stalls, and the grounds are beautiful. You'll like the room we have, too. Townsend's really gone all out for this race. Of course Charlie says he'd rather stay at the stables than in a fancy motel room."

"I'll bet." Ashleigh could just picture the old trainer in his casual, baggy clothes and battered hat.

They talked nonstop for the rest of the drive. The limo stopped near their motel entrance, and the driver waited while Jilly showed Ashleigh their room and Ashleigh quickly changed into jeans and a T-shirt. They returned to the limo for the short trip to the backside. Ashleigh was amazed at the amount of activity in and around the barns as they went in search of Charlie.

"Crazy, huh?" Jilly grinned. "A lot of these horses are stabled here for the whole Belmont season. We've had to get Wonder's workouts in pretty early in the morning to beat a traffic jam on the track. You know Brad's been here nearly all week."

Ashleigh knew. His private school had had graduation two weeks before the Lexington public schools. "I was glad he wasn't hanging around the farm."

"He's been working the Prince himself," Jilly added.

Ashleigh swung around. "He doesn't usually work the Prince at the track. He leaves it to one of the professional riders."

"He must be pretty worried about this race." Jilly toyed with the end of her long braid. "He's taking it really personally, like it's a contest between you and him."

Ashleigh frowned. She wished Brad would get over this thing about her and Wonder.

"He ought to grow up," Jilly said. "Though he's not the only one turning this race into a contest. The handicappers and the press are just as bad. Then there's that bonus money to the horse who gets the most overall Triple Crown points."

"Unless Wonder and the Prince both run really badly in this race," Ashleigh said, "the Townsends will get it either way."

"Right," Jilly agreed. "And it's a lot of money."

Ashleigh rarely thought of the purses Wonder was winning, but Jilly's words reminded her of how valuable the filly had become to the Townsends. And if she won tomorrow, she'd add more than a million dollars to her winnings. "Nothing's going to stop us now, Wonder!" Ashleigh vowed to herself.

One of the first familiar faces they saw as they approached the Townsend Acres' stabling area was Brad's. He barely nodded to the girls as he strode past.

"Looks like he wishes you'd missed the plane," Jilly said, laughing. "He knows Wonder does better when you're around."

Wonder whinnied excitedly when she saw Ashleigh, then pranced around her stall before thrusting her head into the aisle and nudging Ashleigh's shoulder.

Ashleigh wrapped her arms around the filly's neck. "You've been a good girl, I hear. And you're going to show them tomorrow, aren't you?"

"She'll give it her best shot anyway."

Ashleigh turned at the sound of Charlie's gruff voice. "Hi, Charlie. Hi, Terry," she added to the smiling groom who walked up behind Charlie. As soon as Ashleigh turned, Wonder resumed her pacing of the stall.

Charlie glanced at the horse. "She'll settle down

more now you're here. She knows something's up. She's been getting more high-strung all afternoon."

Ashleigh frowned. "She's usually okay until just before the race."

Charlie shrugged. "Could be the excitement. A regular parade going through here. I just took a look around at the rest of the field. That English colt's definitely running—big animal. He's supposed to be a late closer, too."

"Excalibur?" Ashleigh asked.

"That's him. Mercy Man's been training well—put in a real nice workout Wednesday. So did the Prince. He's in top form."

"How about the rest of the field?" Ashleigh asked.

"I hear they just scratched Wanderkill—no forecast for rain tomorrow, and he only did well in the Preakness because of the slop. Sandia's looking tired, and I don't think he can go the mile and a half anyway. Gyro either. The English horse will be our only surprise."

"Jilly said Wonder had a good workout."

"She did. I've got no complaints," Charlie said.

"But the press do," Terry grinned. "Charlie won't tell them anything."

"Dang reporters with their questions."

"You love it," Jilly told him. "You'd be upset if they didn't come by."

"Hmph," Charlie grunted. "No need for them to

know the mile and a half is what we've been training her toward all along."

Ashleigh and Jilly laughed. "You old sneak," Jilly said.

During what remained of the afternoon, Jilly took Ashleigh on a tour of the track. The facilities were everything Jilly had promised. Ashleigh's head was buzzing by the time they all met for a quiet dinner at the track kitchen. She was sure she'd be out like a light as soon as her head touched the pillow that night, but that didn't happen. Jilly slept peacefully in the next bed, but Ashleigh's thoughts were churning. The more she reminded herself that she had to be up at the crack of dawn, the more she tossed and turned. She finally dozed off, then woke suddenly from fitful dreams of Townsend Prince winning and Wonder coming in last . . . the crowds were jeering, and Brad was gloating and telling her Wonder was *his* horse now. Ashleigh barely slept at all after that and was heavy-eyed as she and Jilly dressed to go over to the track.

She forgot her tiredness once she was there. Charlie only wanted to jog Wonder lightly over the track to limber her up, and to Ashleigh's amazement, he told her to ride. The track was congested, but Ashleigh wasn't as nervous as she'd thought she'd be. Nothing really could go wrong when she was cantering the filly only once around the mile-and-a-half oval. Wonder was an absolute handful, though. She refused to settle or concentrate. She fought Ashleigh's gentle pressure on the reins. She was ready to shy at the slightest unexpected noise or shadow. Ashleigh couldn't understand it. The filly had never been so headstrong or unresponsive in their workouts before. Ashleigh felt as if she'd galloped out two miles by the time she rode Wonder off the track. Sweat was pouring down her brow, and her arms and shoulders ached from trying to keep the filly in hand.

Charlie was waiting by the gap, squinting into the sun that was rising over the grandstand behind Ashleigh. "Not good," he said.

"No," Ashleigh breathed. He held Wonder's head while Ashleigh dismounted. As soon as Ashleigh was on the ground, Wonder danced her hindquarters around and nearly collided with a groom holding a horse a few yards away. Charlie quickly led the filly a safe distance away.

"She's acting strange!" Ashleigh said.

"Hold her. Let me untack her," Charlie said as Ashleigh was about to loosen Wonder's girth. While Ashleigh held the filly, Charlie quickly removed the saddle. He flipped it over and examined the pad beneath, then ran his hands carefully over Wonder's back. "I thought something might have got under the saddle pad and was irritating her," he said finally, "but I can't see anything. Take her back to the barn and see if she settles down any. It's got to be all the craziness around here. Those reporters and camera people aren't getting near her stall this afternoon, I'll tell you."

Charlie was true to his word. During the rest of the busy morning hours, he kept all press and curiosity seekers at a distance. Wonder had settled down a little by midafternoon. Terry had given Ashleigh a hand bathing and grooming the filly, and she looked magnificent as Ashleigh put her back in her stall. Her coat gleamed like brightly polished copper. Her mane and tail flowed in silky cascades, and her hooves shone from the oil Ashleigh had applied.

"Could be she's just in a mood," Charlie said, as he joined Ashleigh for the tedious last hour's wait before going to the receiving barn. "Sit with her for a spell." He checked his old pocket watch. "Then you'd better go get yourself cleaned up. Have Terry keep an eye on her while you're gone."

Ashleigh glanced down at her dirty, still-damp jeans and T-shirt. Her hair was a mess, too. Most of it had fallen loose from her ponytail and clung damply to her cheeks and neck. She couldn't lead Wonder in the walking ring looking as she did!

She found Terry before she left to change, and he agreed to stay by the stall. Wonder was quieter and seemed to be dozing in the back of her stall. Ashleigh set out across the backside with her change of clothes.

On her way back to the barn a half hour later, she was stopped by a reporter, who knew of Ashleigh's part in Wonder's career. Ashleigh hurriedly answered a few questions, but she didn't dare say too much. When she arrived at the stall, there was no sign of Terry, and Wonder was no longer a quietly peaceful horse. She was snorting and prancing around her stall.

Terry rushed up a second later, breathless. "Sorry, I was only gone a second. One of the Townsend grooms needed something. What happened?" he exclaimed when he saw Wonder. "She was fine when I left."

"She's been acting strange all day. I think she knows it's getting close to race time." Ashleigh went into the stall, soothed the filly, and looked her over. Wonder seemed fine—physically.

Charlie showed up a moment later, ready to take Wonder to the receiving barn. Wonder practically dragged Ashleigh out of the stall.

"She knows what's coming," Charlie said. "She doesn't like this waiting around any more than we do. She'll sort herself out once we get in the saddling area." But Ashleigh noticed Charlie was scowling. He was as confused by Wonder's behavior as she was.

Wonder's bright copper coat was already dark with sweat as Charlie prepared to saddle her, yet the air temperature was only in the seventies. The filly pulled against the lead shank and swiveled her hindquarters restlessly as Charlie put on her bridle, saddle, and blinkers.

Clay Townsend walked over just in time to see the high jinks. "The filly seems pretty high-strung today," he said to Charlie.

"I don't like it," Charlie muttered. "She's running her race before she even gets on the track."

Mr. Townsend frowned. He was obviously edgy and distracted himself. "She was checked out clean by the vet. She'll settle down once she gets out there. The race is important."

"And we just might blow it, the way she's behaving," Charlie grumbled under his breath. But Townsend was already walking away toward Ken Maddock and Townsend Prince.

"I think Terry better walk with you this time, missy," Charlie said as the grooms prepared to lead the saddled horses to the walking ring. He shook his head as Ashleigh took a firm grip on the lead shank. Terry clipped another to the right side of Wonder's bridle.

"She's wired for sound," Terry murmured to Ashleigh. "What's gotten into her?"

"I wish I knew." Ashleigh laid a hand on Wonder's

neck, hoping to steady her at least a little bit. From the looks cast their way as they circled the ring, Ashleigh could see that others had noticed Wonder's state. She saw people whispering among themselves.

When Jilly and Charlie came into the ring, Jilly's expression was tense. As Charlie gave her a leg up into the saddle, she whispered to Ashleigh and Charlie, "Looks like I'm going to have a handful."

"Don't even try to pace her," Charlie said. "Just let her go and hope she works this mood off. She may have nothing left for the end of the race, but we'll have to risk it. No telling how she'd react if you tried to hold her."

Jilly nodded. Charlie stepped back. The grooms, horses, and jockeys continued around the ring.

Ashleigh had a sick knot in her stomach by the time the horses left the ring for the track. Was the filly sensing the pressure and high hopes everyone was putting on her? But she hadn't acted like this before the Derby or the Preakness.

Ashleigh was lost in thought as she and Charlie made their way to their seats in the grandstand. Her hands were cold as ice as she watched Wonder toe-dance through the post parade and skitter through her warm-up. Even with an escort rider holding the filly, Jilly needed all her skill to keep the filly in line. For the first time Ashleigh was thankful Wonder had drawn one of the outside post positions and wouldn't have to stand long in the gate while the other horses were loaded.

Wonder's coat was totally darkened now with sweat. Ashleigh glanced over at Charlie and saw him shake his head. Ashleigh held her breath and kept her fingers crossed as Wonder loaded in the gate. The remaining two horses loaded quickly after her. There was a second's agonizing wait, then the gates flew open. The race was off.

Wonder exploded like a rocket, straight for the lead. Ashleigh knew that Jilly had her fingers wrapped around both the reins and a chunk of Wonder's mane. Otherwise the filly would have bolted out from under her, leaving Jilly sitting in the dirt at the gate.

Following Charlie's instructions, Jilly made no attempt to stop the filly's headlong flight. Wonder roared down the track on the outside of the field, passing other horses as if they were standing still. She was in the lead by a length before they went into the clubhouse turn. Jilly eased her in closer to the rail.

Ashleigh heard the announcer cry, "Ashleigh's Wonder is setting an incredible pace here! Jilly Gordon's let the filly loose on the lead!"

"Let's hope it doesn't burn her up," Charlie muttered.

"Sandia, expected to go right to the front, is in second. Gyro is running with him. Excalibur is laying in behind, then Dr. Casey, Rhythmic, Townsend Prince, and Mercy Man, biding their time . . ."

Ashleigh watched in stunned amazement as the field moved down the backstretch. Wonder's strides were eating up the track. She had more than a three-length lead on the rest of the field. It was heart stopping to watch her speed as she set track-record fractions—but frightening, too. Wonder was running like a horse out of control. Ashleigh couldn't see how the filly would have anything left at the end. And there was still a lot of race to run.

"The half in forty-three and four," the announcer gasped. "Unbelievable fractions, but can she hold on? The filly's drawn off to a five-length lead! Sandia's holding on to second. Gyro a neck back in third, but Excalibur is moving up quickly on them. Townsend Prince has begun to move up along the outside. He's into fifth. Dr. Casey and Rhythmic inside of him. Mercy Man is in tight quarters behind, looking for an opening. Excalibur has moved into second. Sandia and Gyro are fading. But Ashleigh's Wonder is still roaring on the lead as they head into the far turn."

Ashleigh's heart was racing. How long could Wonder keep up the pace? She glanced over to Charlie. His mouth was set as he riveted his binoculars on the field.

"Rhythmic's looking for room on the rail and not

finding it. Mercy Man is in full stride on the far outside, picking up horses. And now Townsend Prince is being asked to run. He's up into third and gaining on Excalibur, but Ashleigh's Wonder has the lead by a solid eight lengths! We may be watching a history-making race, ladies and gentlemen!"

Ashleigh felt dizzy from the tension. Townsend Prince was in full stride now and moving up fast. Mercy Man was right behind him, surging between horses. Excalibur was holding on to second, but Wonder still had a strong lead. "Please hold on," Ashleigh whispered. "Don't run out of steam."

Suddenly, beside her, she heard Charlie exclaim. She looked back to the rest of the field. Townsend Prince was being eased. The colt had ceased his onslaught. A moment later his jockey started pulling him up, and the rest of the field swept by him on the inside.

"Trouble," Charlie muttered.

"Avery is pulling Townsend Prince up," the announcer shouted. "Looks like the Prince is out of it. Excalibur is still taking up the challenge. Vito has found room on the rail for Rhythmic, and Mercy Man is in full gear on the outside. And *down* the stretch they come! Ashleigh's Wonder hasn't let up. Excalibur is desperately trying to wear down her lead. Mc-Corey is going at him with the whip, but the filly's still flying under a hand ride. No whips are ever carried with this filly. And here comes Mercy Man! Can she hold on today after setting what's looking like a stakes record-breaking pace? She's at the sixteenth pole, and holding on!"

Ashleigh watched in agony as Excalibur slowly began to gain ground. Mercy Man was right behind him, only a neck back. As they approached the wire, Wonder's lead shortened to four lengths, then three, but Wonder dug in again as Jilly glanced back, then kneaded her hands along Wonder's neck.

Ashleigh screamed as the filly approached the wire. "Go! *Go!*"

Wonder powered forward. The colts behind her didn't have a hope. Then she was under the wire. She'd won! She'd won the Belmont!

"The filly's won it!" the announcer gasped. "Excalibur four lengths back in second, Mercy Man in third. A spectacular Belmont! And she's tied the stakes record!"

Ashleigh couldn't move; she couldn't think; she couldn't speak. The whole race seemed like a dream. Wonder's performance was just so fantastically incredible. She felt light-headed, and suddenly she realized her knees were shaking. She reached for Charlie's arm to steady herself.

The old man seemed as stunned as she was. "Something else," he murmured, shaking his head. "Never had a horse I trained run like that." Then he pulled himself out of it. "Let's see what kind of condition she's in coming out of it. Keep your fingers crossed, missy."

As they descended toward the winner's circle, Ashleigh watched Jilly circle the victorious Wonder and jog her back down the track. From the distance, Wonder looked okay—sweated up, but moving smoothly with a jaunty tilt to her proud head.

Mr. Townsend hurried up behind them. "What a race, Charlie! I wouldn't have believed it if I hadn't seen it with my own eyes! The only down spot is the Prince."

"How is he?" Ashleigh asked.

"Brad's with him. From what the vet can tell so far, it looks like a strained tendon. Nothing too serious, thank heavens! It'll keep him out of action for a while, but we've got another horse to congratulate."

They were mobbed as they made their way to the winner's circle. Cameras were pointed in their faces. Reporters yelled for their reactions. Mr. Townsend smiled broadly, "We're delighted—absolutely delighted." He went straight to the officials in the winner's circle, but Ashleigh and Charlie went to Wonder. Terry and an attendant were holding Wonder's reins. Terry and Jilly were grinning from ear to ear. Ashleigh threw an arm around Wonder's sweat-bathed neck and rubbed the filly's velvet nose. "What a girl! I'm proud of you!"

Jilly looked a little pale under her smile as she dismounted and removed the saddle for her after-race weigh-in. "A wild ride," she said quietly to Ashleigh and Charlie. "I don't know what got into her. I couldn't have slowed her if I'd tried. My main fear was that she was going to hurt herself. Amazing. Absolutely amazing."

"She looks okay so far," Charlie said cautiously. Too many people were watching Wonder like hawks for him to be obvious about his concerns. When Jilly went off with the saddle, he said to Ashleigh in an undertone, "She's still too keyed up to show it, but she's beat. She's only running on nerves. I'll know more when we get her back in the barn, but she's going to need a rest after this."

The commotion around them was intense. Terry put another saddle on Wonder's back, and Jilly returned to mount for the ceremonial photos. Despite her exhaustion, Wonder tossed her head as the camera shutters clicked in a flurry. Mr. Townsend motioned for Charlie to join him as the trophy was presented, and a network commentator hurried up to interview the two of them. The media attention didn't stop as Jilly dismounted again, and Ashleigh and Terry draped Wonder in a green and gold Townsend Acres sheet. There was another presentation still to come. Townsend Acres would be awarded the million-dollar bonus check for Wonder's performance in the Triple Crown.

Ashleigh went through it all in a daze. She held the filly, talking to her, praising and soothing her. Finally they were able to lead Wonder off to the backside. Reporters followed them, but Charlie brushed them off. "Not now. Give us a chance to get the filly settled."

Back in the yard Charlie carefully checked the filly over before Ashleigh sponged her down. Wonder whickered gratefully as the cool water coursed over her steaming body and bathed away the lathered sweat from her copper coat. There were still plenty of onlookers, but they kept their distance. Charlie's warning scowl would have scared off even the bravest reporter. There were smiles, too, from some of the backside staff, who called out their congratulations.

But a little while later, as she got ready to walk Wonder, Ashleigh saw Jerry Barns from *The Daily Racing Form* walk over to Charlie and heard him speak quietly to the trainer. "What happened in the paddock?" he asked. "I've never seen her keyed up like that. I thought she was going to blow it."

"Beats me," Charlie frowned.

"Didn't hurt her performance, but there's going to be talk."

"Yup, and I expect they'll be doing blood and urine tests on her, looking for drugs."

"You think it would have been a different race if Townsend Prince had stayed in?"

"Different, sure. But he wouldn't have caught her today." Charlie motioned with his head toward an approaching official. "Here we go. Just like I thought."

5

WONDER CAME THROUGH THE DRUG TESTS WITHOUT A PROBLEM, but there was plenty of talk around the backside that evening. Wonder was exhausted by her effort. She calmed down after Ashleigh had walked and groomed her, but she barely touched her feed. Charlie shook his head when Ashleigh told him. "Not surprising. She ran her heart out."

Mr. Townsend insisted on taking them all out to a lavish, celebratory dinner. Charlie grumbled loudly to Ashleigh and Jilly about having to get decked out to go to a fancy restaurant. Yet once they were all seated, he was soon deep in conversation with several horse owners and trainers Townsend had invited. Everyone had high praise for Wonder, with one exception.

Brad barely spoke to Ashleigh. When she asked him how the Prince was doing, he muttered coldly,

"He'll be fine in a month or two." Then he deliberately turned away from her to talk to the man at his side. Few at the table missed the snub, and Ashleigh saw the looks several people exchanged.

"He acts like it's my fault the Prince went lame," Ashleigh whispered angrily to Jilly, who was sitting next to her.

"You know he can't stand to lose," Jilly said. "Ignore him."

"But it looks so bad," Ashleigh said worriedly.

"*He* looks bad. Not you."

Within a week of their return to Townsend Acres, Wonder was her sweet, affectionate self and was doing everything in her power to please. That puzzled Ashleigh all the more. Had it just been the excitement that had transformed her into a skittish ball of nerves?

"Must have been," Charlie said. "A long campaign. Sometimes each race gets more stressful." Ashleigh frowned, unconvinced.

Townsend Prince was back at the farm, too, recovering from his injury. The outlook for the colt was good. The vet was sure he'd be back in form by the end of summer. But Brad still glared at Ashleigh whenever he saw her in the stable. When his father threw an afternoon party the following weekend to celebrate Wonder and the Prince's success in the Triple Crown, Brad put in a brief appearance, then sped off in his Ferrari with Melinda.

"His tough luck," Linda said to Ashleigh. "He's missing a great party."

That was the truth. A huge striped canopy had been set up in the stable yard, with tables laden with food beneath it. Mr. Townsend had even hired a country-and-western band for entertainment, and anyone who wanted to come was invited. Wonder and Townsend Prince, the guests of honor, were brought out of their stalls and treated to a specially made carrot cake. Ashleigh thought it was wonderful, and so did the two horses, as they gobbled it up and looked for more.

Caro and Justin, her boyfriend, strolled up with full plates. "Guess we have Wonder to thank for this."

"Make sure Brad doesn't hear you say that," Linda said. "Hey, who's that with Jilly? He's cute, and he looks kind of familiar. Wait a minute! Isn't he Townsend Prince's jockey—Craig . . ."

"Avery," Ashleigh acknowledged with a laugh. "That's him."

"Wow. He and Jilly look awfully friendly."

"Why shouldn't they be?" Caro said. "Jilly's a jockey, too, remember. She's bound to know him after riding in the same races."

"He's not married, either," Linda speculated.

"Don't you dare start teasing Jilly," Ashleigh warned.

"Oh, I won't, but wouldn't it be neat if . . ."

Mike caught Ashleigh's eye, and they both laughed. It had been good to come home and see him again, especially after Wonder's upsetting and exciting race. Ashleigh's earlier awkwardness had worn off again, and she was glad he had been able to come to the party.

Caro tapped Ashleigh's shoulder. "Look at Mom and Dad." She motioned to the platform that had been set up for dancing. "They're really going at it! Oh, God, how embarrassing."

Ashleigh was pretty amazed, too, seeing her parents dancing to a fast rock number.

"They're good," Justin said.

"They're not your parents." Caro's face flushed.

Justin grabbed Caro's hand. "Come on, let's go give them some competition."

"No—" Caro started to protest, but Justin was already dragging her off.

One of the young stable grooms came over and bashfully asked Linda if she'd like to dance. Linda was off like a shot. Mike looked at Ashleigh, but Ashleigh was still holding Wonder at the end of the lead shank.

"Later," Mike said. Ashleigh smiled faintly. She wasn't too confident of her dancing abilities—she hadn't had much practice. She had to admit it looked like fun, though.

Wonder pressed her muzzle in Ashleigh's hand, looking for more of the special cake. "No, you've had enough, girl. Besides, you and the Prince ate it all." She glanced over at the chestnut colt being held by his groom a few yards away. The Prince strained his head against his lead. He looked no worse for his injury, although his right foreleg was wrapped in protective bandages. He really was a nice horse, Ashleigh thought, and looked so much like his half sister, Wonder. It was only because of Brad's attitude that she'd never really made friends with the Prince.

She noticed that the Prince's groom was looking her way. "Probably time to bring them in," she said.

"I was thinking the same thing," he answered. "I'd like to get out there and have a little fun myself."

Mike came along as Ashleigh led Wonder back toward her stable building.

"She looks thin," Mike said, "but is she coming along all right otherwise?"

Ashleigh nodded. "The rest is doing her good."

"Well, that was some race she ran. She has an excuse for being tired."

"Even if she ran like she had a swarm of bees chasing her?"

"I wasn't going to say that," Mike said.

"Other people have." Ashleigh frowned and

roughly pushed her hair off her cheek and tucked it behind her ear. "They think there had to be a reason why she was so wired—that we did something."

"Don't worry about what other people think."

They'd reached Wonder's stall, and Ashleigh led the filly in. Automatically, she checked Wonder's hay net and water bucket. They were full. She unclipped the lead shank and patted the filly's shoulder. Wonder gently swung her head around and rubbed it against Ashleigh's. "See you later, sweetie," Ashleigh said.

Wonder whuffed, then went to her hay net. Ashleigh and Mike headed back up the stable aisle. When they stepped outside, the band was just starting another song, a slow dance. Mike touched her elbow. "Let's dance," he said.

Ashleigh swallowed. Mike was bound to be a much better dancer than she, but what the heck. She shrugged and smiled. "Just make believe you don't feel it if I step on your toes."

"You won't do that." Mike laughed.

Ashleigh wasn't so sure, but Mike had taken her hand and was leading her toward the dance platform. She was glad to see that neither her parents, nor Caro and Justin were up there. She did see Jilly and Craig Avery, but they were on the far side and seemed very absorbed in each other.

Mike was relaxed and confident, and Ashleigh

quickly forgot about being self-conscious. She put her hands loosely on Mike's shoulders, and he held her gently by the waist. The music was quiet enough that they could talk, and when Mike started joking about Charlie and all the attention the old trainer was getting, Ashleigh felt much less nervous. "He says he hates it," Mike said, laughing softly, "but look at that crowd around him now."

Ashleigh glanced over at the group standing under the trees around Charlie and nodded, smiling.

"You know the junior prom's next weekend," Mike said unexpectedly. "I was wondering if you'd go with me?"

Ashleigh stared at him. "The . . . the junior prom?" she stuttered.

Mike smiled. "Yeah. I was going to ask you before this, but you were so busy getting ready for the race."

Ashleigh didn't know what to say. Mike was asking her for a real date. And to the *junior prom*? Mike was waiting. She had to give him some kind of an answer. She knew her cheeks were flushing. "Ah . . . I don't know . . . ," she finally said. "I mean I think I'd better ask my parents . . ." Ashleigh knew as she spoke that it was a pretty dumb excuse, but she needed time to think. She liked Mike a lot, but she'd tried not to think about them actually dating, like boyfriend and girlfriend. She'd never even *had* a date before. And to go with him to the junior prom!

Mike seemed to understand her hesitation. He was still smiling. "You don't have to tell me now," he said. "Think about it."

For the rest of the dance, Ashleigh's head was spinning. Mike had asked *her* for a date to the junior prom. She knew he liked talking horses with her, but why hadn't he asked Jennifer Marshall, or one of the other gorgeous girls he knew who were dying to go out with him?

Linda and Caro ganged up on her that night as they were all getting ready for bed—Linda was spending the night. "So what's going on with you and Mike?" Linda said as soon as the bedroom door was closed. Caroline plopped down on the edge of her bed, obviously dying of curiosity, too.

"Nothing," Ashleigh said, digging out her pajamas.

Caroline smiled slyly. "I don't believe it. You've been acting weird ever since you danced with him."

Ashleigh sighed. She knew they wouldn't let up until she told them, and in a way she'd feel better if they knew. "He asked me to the junior prom. I don't think I'm going to go, though."

"What do you mean?" both girls shrieked.

"I wouldn't feel right. I've never been on a date, and to go to the junior prom? There'll be a whole bunch of kids I don't know—all from high school and older than me. I wouldn't know how to act."

"Act like you always do!" Linda cried. "You and Mike always get along great—and you like him."

"I like him a lot . . . but we're just friends."

"So what's wrong with going out with a friend?"

"I don't have anything to wear—"

"Caro can help you find something," Linda said determinedly.

"Right," Caro agreed eagerly. "That's no excuse, and you know it."

Ashleigh looked helplessly at the two of them. "All right, I'm scared," she admitted.

"Well," Linda conceded, "I suppose I'd be pretty nervous if Mike asked me out. But you and Mike do stuff together all the time, and that doesn't scare you."

"This is different," Ashleigh said stubbornly.

"Come on, Ash," Caro pleaded. "You've got to start dating sometime, and Mike's one of the neatest guys you could find."

"We'll help you get ready," Linda coaxed. "Tell him yes, Ash. Can you just picture what Jennifer and Corey will say? They'll be green!"

Ashleigh looked back and forth between them. She probably was being stupid to be so nervous. She wouldn't have thought twice if Mike asked her to go riding with him. On the other hand, she just couldn't picture herself at the prom—she wouldn't feel natural. *But,* she did like Mike, and part of her was excited at the idea of going out with him. Finally she smiled uncertainly. "Okay."

"Yay!" Linda and Caro bounced up and down on the beds.

The next afternoon her mother talked to her. "Caro told me Mike asked you out," Mrs. Griffen said with a smile. "I'm glad you're going. Mike's a nice boy." She put her arm around Ashleigh's shoulder. "I remember how nervous I was about my first date. I ended up having a great time, and so will you."

When Mike called her Monday night, Ashleigh told him she'd go. "Great. I'll pick you up at seven-thirty, okay?"

"Okay," she answered, but she felt her stomach flutter at the thought.

6

CARO AND MR. GRIFFEN HAD ASSURED HER SHE LOOKED WON-
derful in the dress she and Caro had bought in Lexington. It was a deep peach color that brought out the
auburn highlights in Ashleigh's hair and made her
skin glow. And Ashleigh liked what Caroline had
done with her hair, sweeping it up with combs. It
made her look older and showed off her pretty fea-
tures. Mike certainly had given her a surprised and
admiring look when he'd picked her up. But she felt
completely uncomfortable as she looked around the
crowded high school gym.

She hardly knew *anyone*! Having Mike at her side
helped. He looked fantastically handsome in his
white suit, and he sure was popular. Tons of people
came over to the table where they were sitting with
Mike's best friend, Chad, and his girlfriend, Diane.
Mike introduced Ashleigh, but she was so nervous,

she had trouble remembering names. Diane was nice enough, even if she and Ashleigh had absolutely no common interests, and the band was great. She and Mike did a lot of dancing, but when they were on the floor, Ashleigh noticed several girls staring at her and whispering. Their stares made her even more uncomfortable.

Ashleigh tried, for Mike's sake, to pretend she was having fun and to hide her discomfort, but halfway through the evening, when the band was taking a break, Mike leaned over and spoke in Ashleigh's ear. "You're not having a very good time, are you?"

Ashleigh cringed. "Oh, no . . . well . . . it's just that I don't know anyone, I guess . . . I'm sorry."

"Nothing to be sorry about." Mike smiled. "And this dance isn't the greatest. I'm getting pretty bored. Let's go for a ride—maybe get a hamburger or something. Okay?"

Ashleigh hoped her relief wasn't too obvious. But Mike was still smiling, so she smiled back. "I'd like that."

They said good night to Chad and Diane, then set out in Mike's pickup. It was a gorgeous night, warm and bright from a nearly full moon. "You're not mad about leaving early?" Ashleigh asked as Mike wove down Lexington streets.

"No, why should I be?" Mike said with surprise. "I

just want you to have a good time. Besides, with all that dancing, I'm getting pretty hungry."

Ashleigh laughed and relaxed. "Me, too, as a matter of fact."

Mike pulled up to the drive-through window at a fast-food place, and they both ordered hamburgers, fries, and Cokes. "I've got an idea," Mike said. "Let's go back to your place and have a midnight picnic with Wonder. Think anyone would mind?"

"No, I'm sure they wouldn't," Ashleigh said happily. What a great idea, she thought. Mike *was* a special guy.

So half an hour later Wonder had a surprise as two very dressed-up visitors arrived at the semidark stable, pulled up a couple of stools outside her stall door, and cheerfully settled down to eat. Half-asleep when they'd arrived, the filly quickly perked up and not so politely demanded her share of their french fries. The three of them had a wonderful time, Ashleigh and Mike talking horses, and Wonder putting in her two cents with an occasional snort or nicker. The rest of the evening flew by, and Ashleigh couldn't remember why she'd ever felt uncomfortable around Mike. Finally Mike walked Ashleigh up to the door well after midnight. He gave her a chaste kiss on the cheek, but flashed a warm smile. "This is one of the best dates I've had in a long time. Thanks. I'll talk to you soon."

"Thank *you*," Ashleigh said softly, her eyes shining. Her face felt especially warm as she walked upstairs.

Caroline had come home from her own date and was awake when Ashleigh came into their bedroom. "So?" she asked eagerly. "Did you have a good time?"

"Mmmm," Ashleigh smiled secretively. "Very good."

"See, we were right in talking you into going!"

Ashleigh didn't tell her sister that the best part of her evening hadn't been the dance, but the impromptu picnic afterwards.

All the Griffens were in the high school auditorium a week later to watch Caroline's graduation ceremonies. Caroline looked so adult in her cap and gown, and Ashleigh glowed with sisterly pride as Caroline was presented with one of the larger scholarships. Afterward, Ashleigh noticed that both her parents had damp eyes. Her father tried to hide his emotion with unusual brusqueness, but her mother pulled a tissue from her bag and beamed through her tears. "It's just so hard to believe you're so grown-up already," she sighed to Caroline. "Everyone told me I'd get all mushy. I said no . . . but they were right!"

"Well, I'm not leaving yet, Mom." Caroline grinned, a little misty-eyed herself. "You'll have to put up with me for the rest of the summer."

A week later the family gathered again for Ashleigh's much less elaborate ninth-grade graduation. The class didn't wear caps and gowns, but it was still exciting.

"High school next year!" Corey exclaimed as the girls gathered in the hall afterward. "I can't wait!"

"Neither can I," Jennifer agreed. "This year has been so boring!" Linda and Ashleigh exchanged a private grin. They knew what Jennifer was looking forward to—she couldn't wait to be around all the older boys.

"Just think," Corey teased Ashleigh, "you'll see Mike all the time."

Ashleigh frowned. She hated being teased about Mike—and it had gotten much worse since the junior prom. "We'll both be in class most of the time. Anyway, we're just friends."

"Sure," Jennifer sniffed. "You keep saying that, but I don't believe it."

"You just wish he'd asked *you* out," Corey said, laughing. "Guess what. I nearly forgot to tell you! My parents have finally said I can spend the summer at Cape Cod with my cousin . . ."

The others chimed in with their summer plans. Ashleigh knew her summer would center on getting Wonder in shape for the Travers Stakes in Saratoga, but she didn't mind that at all.

Townsend Prince was rapidly recovering from his Belmont injury, but Ken Maddock was cautious about putting the colt back in training too soon. Ashleigh overheard him arguing with Brad as she led Wonder through the stable yard one morning in late June.

"His leg's fine," Brad said. "If we start him back in light training next month, we can have him ready for the Travers in August."

"If you push the colt too fast, you won't have a horse to race this fall. The colt needs most of the summer off. Early fall's plenty of time to prep him for the Breeder's Cup Classic."

"And if we do that," Brad growled, "we can forget any chance of the Prince being picked three-year-old of the year!"

"Have a little patience," Maddock snapped. "The summer off isn't going to cost the colt that much, and he'll be in prime shape for the fall."

"Sure, and what about the filly? She gets a couple more wins under her belt, and what do we look like then—even if the Prince beats her in the Classic?"

"I doubt Charlie will run the filly in the Classic. He's more likely to put her in the Distaff and let her run against fillies and mares."

"My father's already talking about the Classic for the filly. He wants another match race."

Maddock muttered something in answer, but Ashleigh couldn't stop Wonder's walk to listen without being obvious.

Charlie wanted to start working Wonder lightly cross-country. Few of the other Townsend Acres horses were worked over the trails to the extent that Wonder was. Ken Maddock and Jim Jennings didn't think it was necessary, but Charlie was a firm believer in building up a horse's stamina over cross-country terrain. Wonder certainly had benefited from it.

"She seems in fine shape, now that she's rested from the Belmont." Charlie pushed back his hat and scratched his gray head. "Still haven't figured out what went wrong there," he added.

"No, neither have I." Ashleigh frowned. "Maybe it was just too much commotion for her?"

"Didn't seem to bother her until just before the race." Charlie said no more as he tightened the girth on his favored riding horse, the Appaloosa mare, Belle. Mike drove in just as Ashleigh and Charlie were ready to set out.

"Hi!" Ashleigh called as Mike got out of his truck. He'd stopped by several times since the dance and had spent a few hours talking to Charlie and watching as Ashleigh gave Rory a hand with his favorite yearling, Lightning.

"Looks like I've come at the wrong time," Mike said.

"Nope. Ride out with us if you want," Charlie said. "Dominator could use a jog. He's over in the first paddock behind the stable. Go get him and tack him up." This alone was a sign of respect from Charlie. There weren't many he'd ask to join them on a training ride.

Mike beamed a smile. "Thanks!" He hurried off in the direction of the paddock and a few minutes later had the retired bay Thoroughbred tacked up and ready to go. Dominator pranced like a young colt, thrilled to be going out. The old gelding and Wonder touched noses in greeting. They were old friends. Dominator, ridden by either Linda or Jilly, had been Wonder's pace horse and companion throughout her early training.

"Nice day for a ride," Mike said, as they all swung into the saddle. "Not too hot yet."

"Thought you'd be busy working your colts," Charlie said as they set off.

"I already have," Mike said with a grin.

"How's Jazzman coming along?" Ashleigh asked.

"Looks like he'll be ready for that maiden allowance race next month. If he does a halfway decent job, I'll head toward another two-year-old race this summer, then think about the Champagne. I don't want to rush him."

"Smart," Charlie said. "The colt looks darned good

to me, but you don't want to burn him out his first season. You'll have plenty of time."

"What do you think of the two-year-olds Maddock and Jennings have in training here?" Mike asked.

"A couple don't look too bad. I don't see another Townsend Prince in the barn this year, though."

"Or another Ashleigh's Wonder?" Mike teased. Ashleigh smiled and met his eyes.

They'd left the training buildings behind them and were trotting easily along a rise that overlooked the entire farm. The view was incredible, with acres of green white-fenced pastures, broken by small stands of trees and the willow-draped stream where all the Griffens had spent many summer hours.

"I get the feeling Townsend's putting all his eggs in one basket this year," Charlie said, "with Wonder and the Prince, but it's early days yet."

"I'm surprised he hasn't asked you to take on some of the two-year-olds," Mike said.

"Might cause a few ruffled feathers with Maddock," Charlie said, chuckling.

They were all moving along at a comfortable trot as they approached a tree-shaded turn in the trail. Suddenly, out of the blue, a horse and rider came tearing around the bend at a full gallop. Ashleigh and Wonder were slightly to the front of Mike and Charlie. Wonder reared in fright as the galloping horse shot past. Ashleigh made a desperate grab for the filly's mane. She was nearly unseated, but managed to hold on as Wonder shot off up the trail in panic.

In that frightening second, Ashleigh reacted automatically, doing what she could to regain control of the terrified filly. Luckily she hadn't lost the reins, though Wonder's unexpected action had pulled them loose in her hands. She collected them and settled deep in the saddle, but Wonder had her head and wasn't about to stop. "Easy, girl," Ashleigh called in as quiet and steady a tone as she could manage. "There's nothing to be afraid of."

In a corner of her mind, Ashleigh wondered what rider on the farm was crazy enough to send a horse galloping around a blind corner. It had all happened so quickly, she hadn't gotten a clear look. Now Ashleigh knew the trail ahead grew rougher before descending a sharp incline. She couldn't let Wonder go galloping down that incline!

She tightened her grip on the reins, hauling back steadily, talking in a quiet voice. Ashleigh didn't even have time to be afraid. She thought she heard hoofbeats pounding behind them, but she couldn't turn to look. The reins were growing damp from the sweat on Wonder's neck. Then she saw Wonder's ears flick back briefly. "That's a girl," Ashleigh said breathlessly, "there's nothing to be afraid of. Slow it down."

Ashleigh tried to judge the distance before the trail suddenly dipped down. Only a half dozen more strides, but Wonder was slowing—she was beginning to listen. From the corner of her eye, Ashleigh saw Dominator suddenly beside them, and Mike's arm reaching out, grabbing Wonder's rein, helping to pull the filly up.

"Easy, girl, easy," Ashleigh soothed. "Here's old Dominator. That's it, good girl." She sighed as Wonder dropped back into a canter, and a few seconds later into a trot. Wonder flung up her head nervously, but Ashleigh patted the filly's neck, soothing her further. She glanced over to Mike. "Thanks!"

"Any time." He smiled, but it was a tight, angry smile.

Charlie trotted up behind them, looking grim. "Dang kid!" he growled. "Think he'd have more sense—him of all people. I could wring his neck."

"Who was it?" Ashleigh asked.

"Brad," Mike answered. "Though I don't know what horse he was riding. He's out of his mind."

Now that Wonder had safely stopped, reaction set in. Ashleigh felt her hands and knees begin to tremble. It had been close. They might have made it down the grade in one piece, but Wonder might just as likely have injured her legs. Ashleigh couldn't even think what might have happened to her if Wonder had fallen, or thrown her off. The year before, Wonder *had* thrown Ashleigh, and it had taken them both time to recover from the experience.

Charlie hopped off easygoing Belle, strode over to Wonder, and laid a gentle hand on the filly's neck. "Yeah, easy there, little lady. It's just me. Had a little bit more of a workout than we intended today."

Wonder snorted, but relaxed further at the old man's expert and familiar touch. Her muscles trembled, and her snorted breaths were rapid, but she remained calm.

"Doesn't seem to have done herself any harm." He looked up to Ashleigh. "Let's just walk them back, nice and easy. She should be fine, but I'm having a word with that Townsend kid! His father, too."

As Charlie went back to Belle, Ashleigh glanced over at Mike. "You okay?" he asked.

She nodded. She still felt a little shaky, but she was recovering. At least Wonder was all right.

"I wouldn't want to be Brad Townsend right now," Mike whispered, as they turned the horses and followed Charlie and Belle.

"Neither would I," Ashleigh agreed.

7

ASHLEIGH FOUND OUT WHAT HAD HAPPENED LATER THAT AFTER-
noon from Terry Bush, who came up to Wonder's
stall when he was sure no one else was around.

"We had quite a scene here when you were out
riding. Brad's girlfriend broke up with him—"

"Melinda did?" Ashleigh gaped.

"She wasn't too private about it, either. She came
storming into the barn and told him off. Said she was
sick of the way he was acting and had found some
other guy." Terry grinned. "I didn't hear it all. Hank
did, though, and filled me in. But I came up in time to
see Brad pull Nightshade out of his stall, saddle him
up, and tear out of here up the trails."

"So *that's* what happened," Ashleigh said.

"Looks like he got a big dose of his own medicine
—I mean, after what he did to your sister, breaking
up with her in front of all the staff."

"I don't believe it." Ashleigh was stunned. "Is Brad still around the stable?"

Terry shook his head. "He brought Nightshade in all lathered up, handed him to his groom, and took off in his Ferrari. Good thing Maddock wasn't around to see the way that colt came in. He'll have a fit when he hears."

"Maddock isn't the only one who's having a fit. Brad passed us up on the worst part of the trail at a fast gallop. Wonder spooked and nearly ran off with me. Charlie's going to have a few words to say, too."

"Whoa," Terry exclaimed. "Sounds like trouble. Think I'll steer clear of Brad for a while. But the filly's okay?" Terry asked with a worried look into Wonder's stall.

"Yeah, she's okay, thank heavens."

That night after dinner Ashleigh told Caroline what had happened.

"You're kidding!" Caro cried. "She broke up with him? All right! And I thought she'd stick to Brad like glue." Caro smiled grimly. "It serves him right. What a jerk."

In the next few days, Ashleigh stayed as far away from Brad as she could. She'd heard from Charlie that he'd had a word with Mr. Townsend, and Townsend had been furious. Brad was definitely in the doghouse, and when he did show up in the stables, he looked like a thundercloud. Luckily he wasn't around much, since the Prince still wasn't being worked, although Jim Jennings was having Brad exercise a couple of two-year-olds. Ashleigh stayed away from the training oval when Brad was riding, and she had plenty to keep her busy anyway.

Linda came over whenever she could, but she and her father were readying a string of horses that would be racing that summer, and in mid-July they would be heading out for some of the northern tracks. Mike came by, too, excited about Jazzman's prospects in his first race in early July. He invited Ashleigh and Charlie to come to Louisville to watch the race, and they both eagerly agreed.

Jilly was away racing at Belmont, and Ashleigh missed having her around, but Jilly kept in touch and would be back at the farm for a week before the Saratoga season. She also hinted shyly at her budding romance with Craig Avery. "Not that we get to see each other much," she admitted, "since he travels to tracks all over the country, but he's going to be at Saratoga, too."

"Hmph," Charlie grunted when Ashleigh passed on Jilly's news. "Hope she's not going to let men start distracting her."

"Come on, Charlie," Ashleigh said, laughing. She remembered back when Charlie hadn't approved of Jilly as a jockey—just because she was female. He'd changed his tune, now, though. "You know Jilly. That won't happen. She wants to get to the big time. Besides, he's a jockey, too."

"Doesn't make it any better."

On the first weekend in July, Justin picked up Caro, Ashleigh, and Charlie for the trip to Churchill Downs to see Jazzman race.

"My brother and Mike are basket cases," Justin said.

"Well, it *is* the first horse they have racing," Ashleigh told him.

"Yeah, guess I understand how they feel, especially Mike. They've put a lot time and effort in—and money."

Because of an accident on the interstate holding up traffic, they arrived at the track only a half hour before Jazzman's race. They just had time to wave to Mike and Chad in the walking ring before going to the grandstand. Ashleigh crossed her fingers as she watched the horses load into the gate. She hoped for Mike's sake the colt did well. Jazzman certainly looked good in the post parade. With her heart in her throat Ashleigh watched the race go off. It was almost as nerve-racking as watching Wonder's races.

The race was a maiden sprint, only five and a half furlongs, around one turn. But Jazzman gave an incredible performance, powering up on the field to win by five lengths! They all broke out in wild cheers, and even Charlie was smiling as they went down to wait for Mike and Chad outside the winner's circle.

Both boys were beaming, although Jazzman was Mike's particular horse. Ashleigh gave Mike a spontaneous hug of congratulations, which Mike quickly returned.

"Darned good start," Charlie told him. "Impressive." As they all trooped to the backside, Ashleigh noticed the speculative glances cast Jazzman's way. It reminded her of Wonder's first race the year before. She noticed Jim Jennings in the backside crowd, too, scrutinizing them and the colt. But in a moment he moved off to see to a two-year-old Townsend Acres had running in the next race.

The next afternoon in the stables, Brad unexpectedly walked up to her. She didn't want to talk to him, but there was no way she could avoid it.

"So," he said, "I hear your boyfriend's colt won his maiden yesterday. Wonder how much free information he picked up around here?"

"None," Ashleigh shot back. "He's done his own work, and he's not my boyfriend."

"Glad you're smart enough to know he's just been using you."

It took a second for Brad's meaning to sink in, and when it did, he was already sauntering away. Ashleigh glared at his back. "You creep!" she growled under her breath. "You jerk!"

"What was that all about?"

Ashleigh jumped, then turned around to see Jilly standing behind her. Instantly her expression changed from a frown to a broad smile. "Jilly! It's so good to see you! When did you get back?" The two girls hugged.

"An hour ago," Jilly said. "But just for a few days. I've got some more rides at Belmont, then on to Saratoga. So, what *was* that all about?"

Ashleigh explained, and Jilly shook her head. "The only thing good that guy's got going for him is looks and a rich daddy . . . and he does know how to ride a horse," she reluctantly conceded. "I hear his girlfriend broke up with him."

For the next few minutes they caught up on news, then Jilly followed Ashleigh to Wonder's stall to say hello to the filly.

"She looks great now," Jilly said. "When's Charlie planning on sending her up to Saratoga?"

"The end of the month. You'll be up there by then, won't you?"

Jilly nodded and smiled. "I've got some rides lined up with other trainers. I can't believe how many mounts I'm getting offered all of a sudden!"

"What do you expect after winning two of the Triple Crown races?" Ashleigh laughed. "You're getting famous."

"Let's just hope my luck holds out."

During the next weeks Charlie had Ashleigh out on the track before dawn to take advantage of the cooler morning temperatures. Wonder was galloping on the oval again and coming along nicely, but the hot, sticky July days were hard on man and beast.

The Townsends had already left for Saratoga to spend the rest of the summer in their house in that beautiful old town. Ashleigh couldn't have been happier to see Brad depart. The atmosphere in the stables changed completely once he was gone. Everyone seemed to relax, and Ashleigh was better able to concentrate on Wonder's training without Brad watching her every move. Jim Jennings was still on the farm, readying some slow-developing two-year-olds, but fortunately he stayed out of her and Charlie's way.

"I'll be glad to get her up to Saratoga," Charlie said one especially hot morning. They'd worked the filly only lightly, and still she came off the oval badly sweated up. Ashleigh wasn't in much better shape. Her hair was plastered to her head under her helmet, and her shirt was sticking to her. "Bound to be cooler up there," Charlie added. "Forgot to tell you, Townsend called me last night. He's arranged to fly the filly up. I'll be going along to keep her company."

Ashleigh stared at Charlie. "He's flying her up?" she repeated numbly. "But I thought I'd be going along in the van as her groom. He didn't say anything about me?"

Charlie took off his hat and wiped his brow with one of his bright cotton handkerchiefs. "I didn't think of that. I should have. Guess Townsend didn't either. He probably figured Terry would take care of the filly, like he did when you had school."

Terry and several other regular grooms had already left for Saratoga to look after some of the second-string horses. Ashleigh had a sinking feeling in her stomach. She'd been dreaming all summer of going to Saratoga with Wonder!

"Sorry, missy," Charlie said as he saw her expression. "You can't get yourself up there some other way?"

"I don't know. Nobody else is driving up. I've got some money in my savings account, but it's for college. My parents won't let me take any out. And they haven't got any extra money. They keep talking about how much Caro's college is costing, even with the scholarship she won."

"Well, we got a couple days yet. We'll put our thinking caps on."

Ashleigh was miserable for the rest of the afternoon. She didn't even have anyone to talk to. Caroline was at work, waitressing in Lexington, and Linda was in Pennsylvania with her father. She thought about calling Mike, but she'd never called him before. He'd always called her. Finally she went out to the breeding barns and talked to her parents.

They both listened sympathetically. "We just took it for granted you'd be going up with Charlie," her mother said.

"So did I."

"I know it's a big disappointment," her father added, "but what can you do? Townsend's the boss, and if he hasn't offered to pay your way . . ." Her father shrugged helplessly. "We just don't have the extra money, Ashleigh. I'm sorry."

"I didn't think you did."

"It's only for a month, and she'll be racing closer to home in the fall."

Ashleigh nodded. She knew she should try to be grown-up about her disappointment, but she couldn't help feeling her whole summer had just been blown.

Rory had overheard part of the conversation, and he did his best to cheer Ashleigh up. "Come and take Lightning for a walk with me, Ash. I was going to take him to the swimming hole."

Ashleigh gave him a weak smile. "Sure," she said with a sigh.

Mike called just after dinner that night. "Hi," he said cheerfully. "I've been so busy with the colt, I haven't had a chance to stop by. I just wondered how you were doing."

"Well, not great," Ashleigh said. She quickly explained what was wrong.

"Heck, that's no problem," Mike answered. "Come up with us. We decided today to take Jazzman and one of my father's horses up. That's one of the reasons I called—to tell you the news. Good thing I did."

"You and your dad?"

"We figured we'd take turns driving the van, and there's plenty of room."

Ashleigh felt her spirits soar. "I'd love to! Oh, gosh, that would be great! But I think I'd better check with my parents. They don't mind my traveling with Jilly or Charlie, but—"

"Yeah," Mike laughed. "I understand. Go ask them. I'll hold on. And if they want to talk to my father, he's right here."

Ashleigh set down the phone and ran back to the kitchen. In a rush of words, she explained Mike's invitation to her parents.

"Well, if his father's going, too," her mother said.

"But let me talk to him," her father added, "just to make sure your going doesn't create any problems."

Ashleigh stood, chewing her lip as her father talked to Mr. Reese. From the tone of his voice, she began hoping it was going to be okay. It was. He handed her the receiver with a grin. "All set. You can go."

She gave a little yelp of excitement, then put the

phone back to her ear and spoke to Mike. "All right! I'm so excited."

"Me, too. We're planning on leaving on Monday— less traffic, but I'll keep you posted. You already have a place to stay up there?"

"Oh, yeah, with Jilly . . ."

When she and Mike said their good-byes, she hurried out to the kitchen to thank her parents, then ran up the drive to Charlie's small apartment in the staff quarters.

He was sitting outside on a lawn chair, enjoying the evening breeze.

"What's up, missy? You look ready to burst."

"I found a ride, Charlie, with Mike and Mike's father!"

"So they're bringing the colt up. Good. I'll be sure to tell Jilly that you're coming after all."

8

ASHLEIGH STRETCHED HER LEGS AND REPOSITIONED HERSELF ON the narrow drop seat in the cab of the horse van. Mike grinned over at her from the front seat. "Not much longer. I know it's a little cramped."

"It would be a lot worse for you." Ashleigh motioned to his long legs. "I don't mind anyway."

"It's Mike's turn to drive next," Mr. Reese called from behind the wheel. "There's a rest area just ahead. I'll pull in there and we can check the horses and stretch our legs."

Pale light was brightening the sky beyond the windows as they traveled up the New York State Turnpike. They'd driven straight through from Kentucky, with Mike and Mr. Reese taking turns driving. They'd had to stop frequently to check and walk the horses, though, and still had another hour on the turnpike before they reached Saratoga.

"We should get there just about in time to watch the morning workouts," Mike said. "There'll be some interesting horses up here for the Saratoga season."

Ashleigh agreed with a nod. "I'll be glad to see some excitement again. It's been pretty quiet around the farm the last couple of weeks, especially after Charlie and Wonder left."

"Maybe we'll get a chance to see her work."

"I hope so." Ashleigh smiled. She was looking forward to seeing the filly and was anxious to know how she was coming along.

When they at last reached the tree-lined streets of the resort town, the sun was just lifting over the nearby hills, which were more the size of small mountains. There was little traffic at that early hour as they drove by huge old homes toward the track. Mike was now at the wheel, and his father turned to Ashleigh.

"You haven't been here before?" Mr. Reese asked.

"The farthest I've been from Kentucky is when I went to the Belmont."

"You're a few hundred miles north of that now. You'll like Saratoga. Lovely old town, though I haven't been up this way in a few years. I guess Mike told you I used to train a string down in Florida, but this'll be the first time we'll be racing our own horses."

"Pretty exciting, huh, Dad?" Mike said.

"Even at my age."

Mike chuckled and Ashleigh cracked a grin.

It was still fairly quiet on the backside when they found a spot for the van and prepared to unload the horses. Mr. Reese knew his way around and went to make sure everything was set for their stabling. Mike and Ashleigh brought the horses out—Jazzman, and Mr. Reese's allowance horse, Timbo Tam. They walked the horses around the van until Mr. Reese returned and motioned them to follow. The reserved stalls weren't far away, and as they approached, Ashleigh saw signs of increasing stable activity—grooms, riders, and trainers preparing for the morning workouts.

"Let's get your gear and see if we can find Charlie," Mike said when the horses were comfortably settled in their stalls. "Dad told me how to find the Townsend stabling."

Ashleigh felt her excitement growing as they set off. She loved the commotion of the track! Mike was looking excited, too, but then he had as much to look forward to as Ashleigh. They found the Townsend stabling, but most of the horses had left for their morning workouts. Terry Bush was in Wonder's stall freshening the bedding. At Ashleigh's call, he looked up and grinned.

"Hey, you made it. Hi, Mike. Jilly and Charlie just left for the track."

"How's Wonder?" Ashleigh asked.

"Great," Terry said. "She settled right in. She'll be glad to see you, though. She keeps looking around like she's waiting for you."

Ashleigh smiled. "We'll go watch the workout then. See you later."

Terry waved them off, and they headed toward the track area. It was easy to find. All they had to do was follow the line of horses and riders heading in that direction.

"My father described the track to me," Mike said, "but I can't wait to get a firsthand look. Think Charlie will have you do Wonder's workouts now that you're here?"

"I hope," Ashleigh said fervently.

It took them a moment to spy Charlie in the crowd near the gap onto the track. All his attention was concentrated on the track. Ashleigh saw why as she and Mike walked up beside him. Jilly had Wonder going at a smooth gallop along the backside. There were several other horses out on the track, but Wonder was working clear of them—and the filly looked good. Ashleigh didn't interrupt Charlie's concentration. He'd tell them what he thought when he was ready. As Jilly passed the half-mile pole, she dropped down in the saddle and let Wonder out into a fast breeze.

Ashleigh noticed others were watching as the filly opened up. Wonder swept around the turn, flying, but making it look easy. She and Jilly flashed under the wire before Jilly rose in the stirrups again. Charlie lifted his stopwatch and showed the results to Ashleigh and Mike.

"Nice," Mike breathed.

"First time I've clocked a breeze here," Charlie said. "Can't complain about the time." He turned to Ashleigh. "So these guys got you here in one piece. None too soon if you want to try working her here. I'm only going to work her tomorrow and Thursday, then give her a day's rest before the race. She'll be glad to see you."

Ashleigh's face had lit up at Charlie's words, and she grinned. "I'll be glad to see *her*. How's the rest of the Travers field looking?"

Charlie shrugged. "With Townsend Prince out of it, I don't think we'll have much to worry about. We'll see."

As they spoke, Jilly rode Wonder off the track and headed toward them. Ashleigh hurried over. "Hey, girl," she called.

Wonder gave a delighted snort and tossed her head when she saw Ashleigh. As Ashleigh patted the filly's neck, Wonder gently butted her nose on her friend's shoulder and nickered. "You looked great, girl," Ashleigh said with a sigh. "I've missed you this last week. Hi, Jilly."

Jilly smiled down. "I'm glad you made it. You just get here?"

"Less than an hour ago."

"She's been working up to the race real well. What was our time?"

Ashleigh told her, and Jilly's smile widened. Charlie and Mike joined them, and Charlie gave the filly a quick once-over.

"She's barely winded," he said. "She likes the cooler weather up here, but they're saying some hot, sticky stuff's on the way. Let's cool her out."

As they walked back to the barns, Jilly filled Ashleigh in on the news, adding with a blush that she had a date with Craig Avery that night. "You won't mind being in the room alone for a while?" Jilly asked. "I won't be late. And Charlie's room is right next door."

"No, why should I mind? Is he riding in the Travers?" Ashleigh couldn't help asking.

"He's taken over the ride on Mercy Man. I've already told him he'll be eating our dust at the wire again."

When they reached the barns, Mr. Reese joined them, and Mike introduced him to Charlie. The three were soon engrossed in conversation as Ashleigh untacked Wonder. Terry came over to collect the gear, then gave Ashleigh a hand sponging Wonder down.

Ashleigh hadn't slept much during the trip north, and when they went to watch the afternoon's races, she was having trouble keeping her eyes open.

"You're feeling it, too?" Mike said. "At least every-one can have an early night tonight."

The next morning Ashleigh was already awake when Jilly's alarm went off at five, and the two girls dressed and walked to the track. "You could have slept in," Ashleigh said to Jilly.

"Since I'm not working Wonder, I told Maddock I'd help him with a couple of his horses. Have you seen Brad yet? He's been working a two-year-old. It's not another Townsend Prince, but it keeps him busy and out of our hair."

"Good," Ashleigh said. "Sounds like everybody's up here."

"Not Jennings. He's taken a couple of horses to New Hampshire to race."

From the time they reached the barns and found Charlie with Wonder tacked and ready to go, Ash-leigh barely had time to catch her breath. She was a little uneasy about riding at a strange and famous track, but as she and Wonder got ready to go out, she saw Mike on Jazzman, and they ended up galloping through the workout together. Wonder didn't seem to mind the company. She didn't try to force the pace, as she usually did when she saw another horse running beside her. She seemed to understand they were out there only for a light work, but she was glad to have Ashleigh back in the saddle again. She was playful, but quick to listen and try to please when Ashleigh took her in hand.

They slowed the horses to a canter as they came down the center of the backstretch for the second time. A gray horse and rider galloped past on their inside along the rail. Ashleigh recognized the rider: Brad. She watched as he galloped on around the far turn. Mike was watching, too, and when they rode off the track, he said, "That gray colt Brad was breezing is entered in the same race as Jazzman."

"Really? Brad's not going to be happy if you beat him."

"Well, we're going to beat him, aren't we, boy?" Mike patted Jazzman's neck, and the horse snorted his agreement.

"I'm almost beginning to feel sorry for Brad," Ashleigh said. "First the Prince is injured, then his girlfriend breaks up with him, and now his two-year-old's going to get beaten."

"You're not serious?" Mike stared at her.

Ashleigh giggled. "I said *almost.*"

Jazzman was running on Friday, the day before the Travers. Timbo Tam would be running on early Saturday in an ungraded four-year-old allowance race. By late Friday morning Mike was getting a real case of nerves.

"Relax," Charlie told him. "Your getting all uptight isn't going to help your colt win."

"That's easier said than done," Ashleigh said quickly.

Charlie rubbed his bristled chin. "Guess I felt the same when I was just starting out."

Mike laughed. "You mean you're not going to be nervous at all before the Travers tomorrow?"

"Charlie just knows how to hide it," Jilly teased. "The more he clams up, the more worried he is."

"Nah," Charlie barked. "You kids just haven't been around long enough. So you'll be running against one of the farm's colts," he added to Mike. "I've been watching him work. He's coming along, you know."

Mike nodded a little grimly.

"Your colt will take it, if your jock handles him right. Better to pace him some. You've got Grazio riding?"

"Yeah. He rode him when we won at Churchill."

"Good choice. Well, I think I'll take a little stroll. Want to come along?" Charlie asked Mr. Reese, who smiled his agreement.

When the two men were gone, Jilly chuckled. "Charlie will be listening for the latest gossip—not that he'd ever admit it. I'd better get going, too. I'm riding in the first race. If I don't see you before Jazzman runs," she smiled at Mike, "good luck!"

"Thanks," Mike said.

"Maybe you should take a walk, too," Ashleigh suggested. "That's what I usually do. You don't have so much time to think."

"If you'll come with me."

"Sure."

For the next hour they toured every foot of the backside. Ashleigh was continually surprised that she felt almost as comfortable with Mike as she did with Linda or her other girlfriends. She was lucky to have a friend like him.

Ashleigh stayed with Mike until it was time for the horses in Jazzman's race to be taken to the receiving barn. She and Charlie were at the walking ring when the field came out under tack, and both of them studied Jazzman's opponents.

Ashleigh saw Brad standing with Ken Maddock. Brad's colt, Panther, looked good, but she noticed Brad give Jazzman a careful scrutiny.

Then the jockeys were up, and Mike and Mr. Reese joined them as they hurried out to the stand.

"He looks great," Ashleigh told Mike as they watched the field warm up.

Mike was strained, but he smiled at Ashleigh's words. "I'm glad you're here," he said.

"Me, too." Knowing what Mike was feeling, Ashleigh said no more as the horses loaded in the gate. As the last horse went in, she felt Mike's hand reaching for hers. She closed her fingers around his. Then the race was off.

The race was a six-furlong sprint around one turn. As the field moved along the backstretch, Ashleigh saw that Jazzman was in perfect position, three back from the leader. But Brad's colt was in perfect position, too. Brad and Ken Maddock seemed to have the same strategy as Mike—wait until the leader started to tire, then roar past him in the stretch.

The horses remained locked in position as they pounded off the backstretch into the turn. Mike's grip on Ashleigh's hand tightened as the field moved around the turn. She felt every bit of his tension. "Now!" he suddenly whispered hoarsely. "Let him go!"

For several agonizing seconds, nothing seemed to happen. Then gradually Jazzman started gaining. Ashleigh could see the colt change gear. But Brad's colt was starting to move, too, and there was an opening on the rail. She heard Mike groan.

"Come on, Jazzman!" Ashleigh screamed. But Brad's horse wasn't giving up. Stride for stride, nose for nose, the two horses raced down the stretch. It was the kind of finish racing fans love—the crowd was roaring. There seemed no way that Jazzman could beat off his rival. It was going to be a photo finish. Then, just before the wire, the colt gave an extra surge. He went under the wire with half a head in front!

"You won!" Ashleigh cried, looking up to see Mike's astonished face.

"Enough to give an old man a heart attack," Charlie said.

"I know what you mean," Mr. Reese said with a laugh. "What a finish! But that colt's special. Get down to the winner's circle," he said to his son.

Almost in a daze, Mike released Ashleigh's hand. "Right." He was beaming as his father led him off.

"Well, that's a good start to the weekend," Charlie said. "Let's hope the luck holds for tomorrow."

9

THE NEXT MORNING DAWNED HOT AND SULTRY. BY NINE THE temperature was already in the nineties. Ashleigh tied her dark hair on top of her head, but she felt damp tendrils slipping down. She pushed them out of her eyes and off her cheeks.

"Not good." Charlie shook his head when he came by Wonder's stall.

The weather seemed to be bothering the filly, too. Ashleigh had lightly jogged her over the track early that morning. Wonder hadn't listened. Her ears and eyes had been all over the place. Ashleigh had finally gotten Wonder's attention, but the filly wasn't herself coming out of it. She danced through the gap off the track.

"Weather's bothering her," Charlie said, as he grabbed the reins. "We'll keep her as quiet as we can.

Give her a cool bath before you groom her for the race."

"The heat's never seemed to bother her this much before," Ashleigh said.

"It's probably the change. We've had a week of coolish weather, now this."

When Ashleigh returned to bathe and groom the filly, Terry was at the stall. "She's acting strange," he said. "She seemed to be dozing when I went off for my break and to have lunch. Now she's acting like she wants to climb out of the stall."

"Charlie thinks it's the weather, but I don't know." Ashleigh chewed her lip as she studied the nervous filly. Wonder wouldn't even come over to the stall opening, but paced back and forth in the rear of her big box stall. "I was just thinking about the way she acted before the Belmont. She wasn't as bad as this, but she was wired. I was talking to Mike about it."

"What were you talking to Mike about?"

Ashleigh turned as Mike walked up to them. Then Mike noticed the expression on Ashleigh's face. "What's wrong?"

She motioned at Wonder. "She's worse than she was this morning. I don't understand it."

Mike stepped closer. Wonder knew him well, but she retreated farther back in her stall, snorting uneasily. "What does Charlie say?"

"I haven't talked to him since this morning." She

checked her watch. "He should be here in a second, though. She may feel better if I get her out and give her a bath." Ashleigh took Wonder's lead shank from its hook and went into the stall. Wonder stayed back in the stall, whoofing anxiously.

"What's the matter, girl?" Ashleigh asked softly. "Is it the heat? Easy, that's it." Ashleigh reached Wonder's side and laid a gentle hand on the filly's neck. Quickly she snapped the lead shank to Wonder's halter. "We'll go outside and give you a bath . . . cool you down a little. Come on, girl."

At first Wonder balked. Hardly believing what was happening, Ashleigh coaxed her, and finally the filly followed. As Ashleigh led her from the stall, Wonder's ears flicked nervously. She looked wide-eyed down the aisle and pranced at the end of the lead.

"Looks like you and Terry may need a hand," Mike said softly.

Ashleigh seriously didn't think she would, but she was glad for Mike's company. She led Wonder out into the shaded yard where a few other grooms were bathing horses. Others were leading horses who were heading to or returning from a race. While Terry held the filly, Ashleigh sponged her down with tepid water, then shampooed her already gleaming coat.

The water and Ashleigh's gentle touch seemed to help. Ashleigh could see the filly begin to relax. "That's what you needed, isn't it?" Ashleigh said, as she worked her hands in massaging motions.

Charlie strode up, taking off his hat and wiping his forehead with his bandanna. "How's she doing?"

"Better now, but she wasn't too good a half hour ago."

Charlie scowled. "Gotta be the heat. She licked her feed pail clean last night, and I had the vet look her over just an hour ago. Said she was fit as a fiddle."

Ashleigh lifted the hose and sluiced water over Wonder's back, rinsing away the soap. She used a sweat strap to get rid of most of the remaining moisture, then went over the filly's coat with soft towels. Wonder seemed in much better shape. She even craned her head around to affectionately lip Ashleigh's shoulder—like her old self.

Ashleigh was relieved as she led Wonder back to the barn to complete the filly's grooming. Charlie was looking a little happier, too. When they reached the stall, Ken Maddock came over to speak to Terry.

"I've got a sick groom," Maddock said. "Could you give me a hand with Mambo? I'm really in a bind. We're already shorthanded."

"Go on," Charlie motioned to Terry. "We'll manage with the filly." A few minutes later Charlie nodded to Ashleigh. "Seems herself again. I've got a couple things to see to. I'll be back before she goes to the receiving barn."

Mike stayed with Ashleigh, talking comfortably as she finished grooming Wonder. Then he had to go off to give his father a hand getting Timbo Tam ready for his race.

"I'll see you at the walking ring," he told Ashleigh. She smiled. "Tell your dad I said good luck."

Ashleigh threw a light, netted sheet over the filly to protect her gleaming coat, then put her back in her stall. She hugged Wonder's head and gave her a kiss. "You'll be okay? I have to go change, but Charlie'll be here in a second."

The filly nickered, quieter now. Ashleigh grabbed her backpack containing her change of clothes and hurried off toward one of the bathrooms. Her clothes were soaked from giving Wonder her bath. She changed into clean pants and a cotton T-shirt, then brushed her damp hair up on top of her head and held it with an elastic band. Gathering up her dirty clothes, she headed back to the stall.

There was no sign of Charlie yet, although there were plenty of people roaming around the barns. She dropped her dirty clothes into the tack box, then checked on Wonder.

The filly was pacing at the back again and had broken out into a sweat. Ashleigh rushed inside. *I shouldn't have left her,* she thought. And where was Charlie? He should have been back by now! "Easy, girl," she said aloud, reaching out her hand to the filly. Wonder snorted loudly but let Ashleigh approach. Ashleigh ran a hand over Wonder's neck. It was soaking wet. There was no time to give her another sponge-down, either. "There's nothing to be upset about," she soothed. But the filly wouldn't relax.

Ashleigh was beside herself by the time Charlie arrived at the stall. He took one look at Wonder and quickly let himself inside. "What happened?"

"I don't know," Ashleigh told him. "She seemed fine, and I went to change. I wasn't gone more than five minutes, but when I got back, she was a mess again. I shouldn't have left her."

"Never bothered her before." Charlie pushed his hat back and scowled. "Don't understand what's got into her. Take her out of the stall. It's just about time to take her to the receiving barn anyway."

Ashleigh continued to soothe Wonder, but it didn't do much good. The filly flung up her head as Ashleigh tried to lead her forward. Once out in the aisle, she danced her hindquarters around, nearly knocking Charlie over. He laid a hand on the filly's rump, steadying her.

For the first time in Ashleigh's memory, the old

trainer looked baffled. "Easy, there, little lady. Wish you could talk and tell us what's up."

As the two of them concentrated on quieting the fractious filly, Clay Townsend walked over. He quickly took in the scene. "She's acting up?" he asked Charlie.

"She's a mess, and I don't know why."

Mr. Townsend was silent. He studied Wonder. "You've got nearly an hour before race time. She'll calm down in the receiving barn."

"And she may not."

"But she was overexcited before the Belmont," Townsend said reassuringly, "and look at the race she put in. She'll get to business once she's out there. She always does. I'll see you in the saddling area."

Charlie nodded absently. All his attention was on the filly. "If I didn't know better, I'd say she was spooked," he muttered. "Can't be, though. Get her stuff, and let's get going. She just might calm down with a change of scene."

Wonder was only slightly better an hour later as Ashleigh led her into the walking ring. Ashleigh just didn't understand it, and her efforts to relax the horse were having no effect. Even with blinkers blocking her view of the crowd, Wonder flung up her head, snorted, and jerked on the end of her lead. She was sweating again, but so were several other horses in the field. They were bound to, with the heat. Ashleigh saw Mike watching, and she saw the worried look on his face.

When Charlie and Jilly came into the ring, Jilly's expression was tightly serious. Charlie gave her a leg into the saddle.

"Looks like you're going to have another ride like the Belmont," Charlie told her. "So be prepared up front."

Jilly picked up the reins. "I'll try to calm her down on the way out. She settles once she's on the track."

Ashleigh held Wonder's head for a second and dropped a kiss on the filly's nose. "You'll be all right, girl," she whispered. Then Jilly and Wonder headed off.

What Ashleigh saw from their grandstand box wasn't reassuring. Wonder toe-danced through the post parade. Ashleigh could see Jilly running a soothing hand over Wonder's neck and knew that Jilly was talking to the filly. It didn't seem to be helping. Wonder balked going into the gate, totally unlike herself, and once inside, she fidgeted. Ashleigh was feeling more and more a terrible sense of foreboding.

The race went off, but Wonder wasn't concentrating. She was off half a beat late, but Jilly quickly steadied the filly. Ashleigh gasped a sigh of relief as

Wonder collected herself and caught up with the rest of the field.

Jilly kept her to the outside, avoiding the congestion of the pack that trailed behind the pacesetters. Trailing the field wasn't Wonder's style, and Ashleigh saw the filly fighting her way up on the outside. Jilly was trying to pace her onslaught, but she wasn't having much success.

The field roared down the backstretch. Ashleigh's eyes were on Wonder. She paid no attention to the leaders, or to the announcer's voice. Wonder was running about five lengths off the leaders, and four wide as the field approached the far turn. Ashleigh saw Jilly give Wonder more rein, preparing for the burst of speed she'd need in the stretch to catch and pass the leaders.

Other jockeys were preparing, too, positioning their mounts, going for their whips. Wonder had drawn up to run a neck behind the fourth runner. The leaders were weakening, and Ashleigh knew Wonder hadn't hit top gear yet. She could still win it!

Then, suddenly, everything fell apart. Ashleigh gasped as Wonder swerved out and reared. Caught unaware, Jilly went flying head over heels to land in the dirt, and Wonder shot off out of control, reins flapping, up the track. It all happened so fast, for an instant Ashleigh, Charlie, and Mike just stared.

"Oh, my God," Ashleigh breathed.

The rest of the field swept into the stretch. Jilly's small form was sprawled, unmoving, near the outside rail. Wonder was racing along, riderless, toward the finish line.

"Jilly," Ashleigh gasped, clutching Mike's hand with white knuckles.

Charlie was already in motion, pushing out of the box. Ashleigh dazedly watched as an ambulance sped out to Jilly's crumpled form. Mike put an arm around her shoulders. "Come on," he said gently.

Numbly, she followed. It didn't seem real. This couldn't be happening. Not Jilly. Anyone but Jilly. As they pushed down the stairs, she saw an outrider catch Wonder and slowly bring the filly under control. Then her view was blocked by the crowd. She heard some of the announcer's words. "Mercy Man, the winner . . . it's uncertain what happened to Ashleigh's Wonder . . . we're told Jilly Gordon is conscious . . ."

Mike was urging Ashleigh along, following Charlie. She didn't know where they were headed, but she was glad Mike was there. All she could think about was that terrible scene—Wonder rearing . . . Jilly flying through the air. Through the hushed commotion of the crowd, Ashleigh could hear the ambulance start its siren. *It must be taking Jilly to the hospital*, Ashleigh thought. *Please let her be okay.*

At last they reached Charlie. The outrider was leading Wonder off the track, and Charlie rushed over to the horse. Several track officials joined him. She could see Charlie talking to them, but the trainer was more interested in checking over the trembling filly.

One look at Wonder, and Ashleigh snapped to her senses. She moved forward with Mike beside her and went to the horse. She took the reins and rubbed her hand over the terrified filly's neck. "Okay, girl. It's going to be all right. It's not your fault. Easy now."

Wonder flicked her ears forward, listening, but her eyes were wide and rolling, and she heaved breaths through her delicate nostrils.

"No obvious injuries," Charlie was saying. "Know more when the vet checks her over." He turned to one of the officials, who held a hand communicator to his ear. "How's Jilly?"

"In pain. Looks like she'll be okay, though, aside from a broken leg. She's talking to the attendants. Says the next jockey's crop spooked the filly. We'll know more when we look at the films."

Ashleigh closed her eyes. A broken leg . . . but it could have been worse. But Jilly would definitely not be racing for a while.

The commotion was increasing. Reporters and curious spectators crowded around. Mr. Townsend squeezed through and went to Charlie and the officials. Ashleigh couldn't hear what they were saying, but finally a path was cleared, and they were able to lead Wonder off.

"Will there be an inquiry?" Mike asked Charlie.

"Yup."

"You think Jilly was right about interference, then?"

"We'll have to wait and see," Charlie scowled.

The vet gave Wonder a thorough check. "The tests look clean, Charlie," he said. "Not a thing wrong with her that I can see, except that she's a pretty tired filly. She's probably not going to eat much, but give her a good rubdown. I'll check on her later."

Charlie nodded. Ashleigh noticed his scowl had grown deeper and deeper as the hours passed.

They visited Jilly late that afternoon at the local hospital. Mr. Townsend had arranged for a private room, and already vases of flowers covered every flat surface. The largest arrangement of pink and white roses was on the nightstand beside Jilly's bed. Its card read, "Craig."

Jilly was propped on the pillows, looking pale and tired. Her right leg was partially enveloped in a plaster cast. She smiled faintly at Ashleigh, Mike, and Charlie as they approached the bed. "If I'm a little spacey, it's because of the painkillers," she told them.

"We've been worried," Charlie said gruffly. "That was a bad spill."

"I'll be back in the saddle in no time." Jilly tried to sound cheerful. "My first broken bone—guess that's a milestone for a jockey."

Ashleigh decided Jilly must be filled with painkillers to be taking it so calmly. The roses next to the bed may have helped, too.

"No one will tell me what happened after I fell, though," Jilly complained. "How's Wonder?"

"Better than you," Charlie quipped.

"No, seriously."

"He is serious," Ashleigh said. "She's shaken up, but she's not hurt. The vet checked her over."

Jilly frowned. "I know what happened. I kept trying to tell them in the ambulance, but they wouldn't listen. The jock on the three horse right-handed his whip. We were just far enough back and in tight enough quarters that it must have whipped right in front of her eyes."

"That would explain it," Charlie said, "considering the state she was in before the race."

"It may even have hit her." Jilly tried to remember. "But I couldn't see that. I just saw it coming—and then, boom!"

"Filly probably would have been all right, if she hadn't gone into the race all out of sorts," Charlie said. "The stewards will be looking at the replays. I'll

115

take a look at them myself. You're the one we're worried about now. I hear you have to hang around here for another day or two."

Jilly nodded. "The doctor's worried about a concussion. I think I'm okay, though. Townsend's flying me back to the farm when I get out." She seemed disappointed. Ashleigh knew Craig was staying in Saratoga to finish out the season—he and Jilly would be separated.

"She'll be out longer than she thinks," Charlie said as they walked down the hall after their visit. "Takes a while for a leg to mend."

For the first time Ashleigh thought of what Jilly's injury meant in the long term. They had some big races planned during the next months, but Wonder was without a jockey.

10

THAT EVENING ASHLEIGH AND MIKE SAT ON THE DECK OUTSIDE Mike's motel room sharing a pizza. Mr. Reese and Charlie had walked back to the barns together to check the horses. Ashleigh leaned back against the railings and realized how tired she was.

"I feel so awful about Jilly," she sighed. "Everything was going so well for her. And now she'll be out for months! She's going to hate it."

"Jilly doesn't blame you," Mike said.

"Oh, I know. It's just that if Wonder had been acting like her normal self, this wouldn't have happened. What's wrong with her? Do you think she's all of a sudden decided she doesn't want to race?"

Mike picked up another piece of pizza from the box between them. "Then why would she train so well? You never have any problems when you work her on the track. If she didn't like what she was doing, it would show up in training."

"Maybe she's just tired," Ashleigh said. "Though she's had two months off since the Belmont."

"She's had a long campaign, Ash, and it could have something to do with the weather, too."

Ashleigh put her half-eaten slice back in the box. She wasn't very hungry after all. "I hope that's all it is. She'll have time to rest before the fall races. But what are we going to do about a jockey?"

"There are plenty of good jockeys around who'd jump at the chance to ride the filly. With Townsend Prince still out of commission, Craig Avery might be interested."

"I don't suppose Jilly would mind her boyfriend taking her place," Ashleigh said with a smile. "And he's good. The problem with a new jockey is Wonder. She's had some bad experiences with male riders. She ended up pulling her shoulder and bruising her ankle the last time Brad rode her."

"Yeah, but not all guys ride like Brad."

They heard voices in the other room, and a moment later Charlie and Mr. Reese came out onto the deck. Neither of them looked happy.

"Found out what might have been part of the filly's problem," Charlie said abruptly.

Ashleigh sat up. "What?"

"Pulaski, one of the grooms from down the barn,

came up to me tonight. After what happened in the race today, he started thinking and remembered seeing a guy waving a crop near the filly's stall earlier today."

"Why didn't he tell you?" Ashleigh gasped.

"Said he didn't think anything of it at the time," Charlie growled. "He didn't know the filly was whip shy."

"Did he recognize the guy?" Mike asked.

"Nope. He remembers him being well dressed, maybe in his thirties. The fella was sort of playing with the crop, slapping it against his hand—nervous habit kind of thing. Pulaski didn't know how long he'd been there, and as soon as Pulaski showed up, the guy beat it. At the time, Pulaski thought he was a guest of one of the owners or trainers." Charlie pulled up a deck chair and sat down. "Having someone swing a crop in front of her would be enough to set the filly off—bring back all those old associations. Especially if the guy had been there for a while."

"An accident?" Mike asked.

"I'd like to think so," Charlie scowled. "The alternative is that we've got a real lowlife around here. Personally, I can't believe it of any of the trainers. Just not worth it. You'd be finished if you got caught doing something like that. I had the groom tell his story to the stewards, though."

"At least we know why Wonder was acting up," Ashleigh said. The news bothered her—a lot.

"We *think* we know," Charlie corrected.

"It does explain why she went wild when she saw a crop flying in her face during the race," Mike said.

Charlie rubbed his gnarled hands down his thighs and frowned. "Let's see how she is when we get her back to the farm. We'll need to start thinking of an alternate jock, too. I've already had a couple of the top jockeys' agents approach me."

Charlie's comment hit Ashleigh like a dash of cold water. She looked down, hiding her expression from the others. She had never had any problems with the idea of Jilly riding Wonder. Jilly knew exactly how to handle Wonder and had the light, gentle touch the filly needed. She didn't like the idea of a stranger riding her filly. But what other choice did Charlie have?

Early the next morning Ashleigh and Mike went to visit Jilly again. The jockey was even paler than the day before and feeling more aches and pains from her fall. But she was trying to keep her spirits up. Her eyes flashed angrily, though, when Mike and Ashleigh told her about the visitor with the crop.

"So thanks to him, I'm here! Well, I don't intend to be out of commission long!" she said in a determined voice. "I sure hope they catch that guy and find out what he thought he was doing! Hey, before you leave, how about signing my cast? I'm going to keep it—

along with all my winning trophies," she said with a brave smile.

Mike and Ashleigh scribbled their get-well-quick wishes. Ashleigh noticed that Craig Avery had already signed, with hugs and kisses. She smiled and winked at Jilly, who gave her a shy grin back.

While Mike helped his father ready the van for their return trip, Ashleigh spent time with Wonder. The filly's ordeal had taken its toll. She'd barely touched her feed, and she was sulking warily in the back of her stall. She gazed at Ashleigh with sad eyes, as if she knew she'd done something terrible the day before and was ashamed.

Ashleigh felt sick—and angry at the man who had been stupid enough to walk around a stable swinging a crop! It was so unfair.

Charlie came up to her as she was saying good-bye to Wonder, and laid a hand on Ashleigh's shoulder. "Don't worry, missy. She'll pick right up once we get her back home."

"I hope so," Ashleigh said with a sigh.

An hour later she left with Mike and his father for Kentucky. Charlie and Wonder would be flying down the following day.

A concerned welcoming party was waiting when the Reeses' van drew into Townsend Acres the next afternoon. Ashleigh's family greeted her with hugs and worried questions. Linda was there, back from her trip with her father, and all the stable hands were anxious to hear the details of the accident and news of Jilly. There were congratulations for Mike, too.

"Come in and have something to eat," Mrs. Griffen offered the Reeses.

"Thanks," Mr. Reese said, smiling, "but we'd better get these horses home and unloaded. How about a rain check?"

Mike drew Ashleigh aside before they left. "It's been a crazy week," he said softly. "I hope you had a good time anyway."

"You know I did," Ashleigh answered.

"I'll come over tomorrow morning, okay?"

Ashleigh nodded, feeling her cheeks flush under Mike's gaze, especially because she knew her parents, sister, and Linda were watching. Mike squeezed her hand. "I'll be over early."

"Okay," Ashleigh said.

Mrs. Griffen already had the makings for sandwiches laid out on the kitchen table. "I'm so glad you're back," she said to Ashleigh. "I can't tell you how your father and I felt watching that race on television. I think it was worse being hundreds of miles away! But Jilly will be all right?"

"She'll be home in a few days. She won't be riding for a while, though."

"And Wonder?"

"Charlie thinks she'll settle down when she gets back."

"It wasn't Wonder's fault, Ash," Rory cried.

"No, it wasn't her fault."

Within a week all the staff and horses who'd been in Saratoga returned to the farm. Jilly was well enough to sit out in the sun and watch the work in the stable yard. She'd quickly learned to get around on crutches, though she complained to Ashleigh that the cast kept getting in her way.

Ashleigh couldn't help noticing that Brad was in a much more cheerful mood.

"The gossip is that he's found a new girlfriend," Jilly told Ashleigh. "Another rich one, though I haven't seen her. Craig saw them together."

Ashleigh had other ideas about Brad's mood change. It was mean, but she couldn't help thinking that Wonder's catastrophe had cheered him up. Not that she thought he was happy about Jilly's fall, but Wonder had been getting mixed press since her behavior at the Travers in Saratoga. Race people were beginning to speculate on the filly's reliability, and to look back at Townsend Prince as that year's star.

There was plenty of speculation around the farm as well. Mike was with Ashleigh when they overheard Jim Jennings talking to some of the exercise riders. "I said all along that filly was unpredictable. Just lucky nothing happened before now."

"What's that guy's problem?" Mike asked Ashleigh.

"Well, when Charlie was able to turn Wonder around, after her early training problems, Jennings looked pretty bad. He'd written her off and told Townsend not to bother racing her."

Mike lifted his brows. "You'd think he would have gotten over it by now. Has Townsend said any more about the filly's fall campaign?"

"Charlie said they had a long talk yesterday. Mr. Townsend wants to start looking for another jockey. He hasn't changed his mind about the Breeder's Cup."

"But you don't really want her to run with another jockey."

Ashleigh stared up at him. "How'd you know?"

"I'd feel the same about Jazzman if I wasn't sure about the rider."

"I'm being selfish, I guess." Ashleigh frowned. "I just don't want some stranger riding her. It's dumb, because no decent jockey would deliberately hurt her. And at least Mr. Townsend knows now that she needs a special kind of jock."

"You'd like to ride her yourself," Mike guessed.

Again Ashleigh shot Mike a look. It was amazing

how in tune they were, how well he seemed to understand her. "Yes," she admitted, "but there's no chance of that happening. No one would let me."

Charlie started regularly working Wonder two weeks later. They'd given her a complete rest, putting her out in the paddock during the day, and it had worked miracles. She'd put on weight and was showing her natural sweet temperament and curiosity. And when Ashleigh worked her, the filly was alert, doing everything in her power to make amends for the accident.

With Wonder behaving so beautifully, it was easy to look back at the incident as just one of those freak things. The stewards' investigation at Saratoga had uncovered nothing to indicate it was deliberate. Jilly certainly bore no grudge against the filly. She came out to the oval on her crutches to watch Wonder work and spent a lot of time by the filly's stall. Wonder seemed to act especially sweet and gentle toward her now.

There was a constant stream of new gossip around the stable, too. Townsend Prince was ready to start training again and was looking fantastic. One of the farm's two-year-olds was making an impressive start and looked as if he might be Derby material. And Brad definitely did have a new and very attractive girlfriend.

"What she sees in him, I'll never know," Jilly said as she, Charlie, and Ashleigh watched the two of them ride out one afternoon.

"No accounting for taste," Charlie said.

Two days later Craig Avery arrived at the farm. Jilly was overjoyed. The two of them were like lovebirds, spending every free minute together. Ashleigh thought Jilly was the sole reason for his visit until Charlie told her that they were going to try Craig on Wonder.

"He's Townsend Prince's jockey," Ashleigh protested.

"True, but we've got to try her out with a new jock sometime. Craig's here, and it'll give us an idea how she handles with a male rider. She'll have to run at least one prep race before the Breeder's Cup, and I don't like being up in the air about a jock."

Charlie didn't look entirely happy either, but Ashleigh knew they had to resign themselves to what had to be. And if anyone was going to try Wonder, Craig was the best choice. He was good, and he didn't try to muscle his mounts around.

"Don't worry," Jilly said as Craig rode out on the oval. "I told him everything I could about the filly. He knows exactly what she likes and doesn't like."

Still, Ashleigh felt a pang as Craig warmed Wonder up. The filly was skittish and uneasy with a new rider

126

on her back. She didn't seem to like it one bit, although Craig was doing all the right things, sitting quietly, talking to her, and giving her a chance to settle down.

"That's it. Nice and slow," Charlie muttered.

But the workout didn't go that well. There were no fireworks. Wonder obeyed—she jogged, she galloped —but she never kicked in.

Craig shook his head as he rode off the track. "We're not connecting. She's a nice filly, beautiful movement, but she doesn't want to put out for me. I don't know what to tell you."

Charlie rubbed his jaw. "Afraid this might happen."

"I wouldn't be taking the mount on her anyway, since I'm committed to ride the Prince in the Breeder's Cup Classic. And I don't even know who to suggest. Most of the big jocks are committed to mounts already, like me."

He swung from the saddle, then turned to Ashleigh, who was holding Wonder's reins. "Why don't you ride her? No, I'm serious. I saw you work her yesterday."

"I—I . . ." Ashleigh stumbled. "They'd never let me. I don't even have an apprentice license or anything—"

"You can get one."

Ashleigh glanced at Charlie and noticed that his

blue eyes were twinkling. "You think I could?" she said with a gasp.

"Oh, I've thought of it, missy. But like you say, I doubt anyone else would be too keen on it. Too much of a risk—you're too young. I can't see Townsend or your parents going for the idea."

"Too bad," Craig said. "It'd be the perfect solution. Well, I'll keep my ears open. There's a decent female jock who rides at the Meadowlands. Sue Wallace."

At the mention of the other girl's name, Jilly frowned.

Craig saw it and laughed. "Just a suggestion. I don't know if she's up to riding the filly anyway."

"Let me know if you get any brainstorms," Charlie said. "Townsend's starting to get anxious. Everyone's buzzing about the Breeder's Cup—wanting another match race between Wonder and the Prince in the Classic. But if we don't get the right jock—" He shrugged.

As Jilly and Craig walked away, Charlie mumbled under his breath. "Persnickety horseflesh!"

"You're disgusted with Wonder," Ashleigh said in a small voice.

"Naw." He patted the filly's neck. "She's a special animal and deserves special treatment. It would just make my life easier right now if she wasn't so fussy. Either that, or you were a few years older."

11

IN LATE AUGUST, CAROLINE LEFT FOR COLLEGE. ASHLEIGH missed her far more than she'd expected. The bedroom seemed so empty—and so quiet. Finally it was the night before high school started, and Ashleigh spent a lot of time on the phone with Linda. They were both feeling nervous and excited about their first day among so many new people. Yet it turned out to be not nearly as scary as either of them had feared.

They didn't have the same homeroom that year, but they knew most of the kids in their class. Best of all, Ashleigh and Mike now went to the same school. Mike met them when they got to the building and walked them to their homerooms. It was so nice having him there, Ashleigh thought. At lunch they sat with Corey and Jennifer, who jabbered nonstop, both of them feeling right at home. Jennifer was already checking out the junior and senior boys. Ashleigh noticed Jennifer getting some interested looks in return.

After school Mike offered to give them a ride home. Linda gave a mean giggle when she saw Jennifer glaring at them as they climbed into Mike's truck.

"Looks like you guys made it through okay," Mike said as he swung out of the parking lot.

"Not bad," Ashleigh answered. "I've got great teachers, except for Mr. Schwartz in English. Caro warned me about him."

Mike smiled. "I had him, too. Just be ready for a lot of surprise quizzes, and you'll do okay."

"I'm glad I didn't get him," Linda said. "I *hate* surprise quizzes. Do you know the tennis coach has already talked to me about being on the team?"

"And why not?" Ashleigh told her. "You were one of the best players last year."

Of course, the conversation soon turned to horses. "When are you racing your colt again?" Linda asked Mike.

"I'm thinking about the Champagne at Belmont early next month. He seems to be training up to it, although I might be running against Brad's colt, Panther."

"If the Prince keeps coming along," Ashleigh added, "they want to run him in the Jockey Club Gold Cup at Belmont that same weekend."

"Has Charlie made any decisions about Wonder's next race?" Mike asked.

"He's thinking of going to Keeneland for either the Fayette at the beginning of October, or the Spinster the week after. He wants to keep Wonder close to home, especially with the Breeder's Cup being held at Churchill Downs this year."

"It'll be like Derby week all over," Linda raved. "I can't wait! You know, my father may even have an entrant for the mile turf race this year."

"You didn't tell me!" Ashleigh cried.

Linda gave a secretive smile. "I didn't want to say anything. We weren't sure. It still depends on how the horse does this weekend, but I think he's got a shot."

"That's terrific!" Ashleigh smiled. "Both of us with horses running!" Then she sobered. "If we can get a decent jockey for Wonder, that is. Charlie and Craig are still looking."

Mike glanced over at her, then looked back to the road. "You'd have a good chance if you rode."

Ashleigh hadn't forgotten about Craig Avery's suggestion—she thought about it all the time. But it seemed like such an impossible dream, she hadn't wanted to talk about it. She hadn't even told Linda or Mike. Now she confessed.

"Craig said the same thing after he rode Wonder," she said softly.

Linda gaped at her. "He did?"

"But you know no one would let me."

"There'd be obstacles all right," Mike agreed. "What does Charlie say?"

"I think he'd like me to ride, but he doesn't think Mr. Townsend would go for it either."

Mike was silent for a moment. "Maybe it wouldn't hurt for you to talk to Townsend anyway."

"Yes!" Linda nodded. "You should! Remember when you didn't think they'd let you train her, and they did? You never would have had a chance if you hadn't asked."

Ashleigh agreed, but if she *did* ask Mr. Townsend and he said no, then she wouldn't have even the slightest hope to cling to. Now, at least, she did. And they still might find the right professional jockey.

Everyone at the farm seemed to be finding excuses to be at the oval in the mornings to watch Wonder and the Prince's workouts. The tension and excitement were growing, but few could make up their minds who was the better horse, particularly since Wonder would have a new jockey. The Prince was coming back to form impressively, and Wonder was training like a dream.

Ashleigh noticed Jim Jennings clocking all of Wonder's breezes, then chatting chummily to Brad afterward.

"Jennings is doing a lot of talking," Hank told her

and Charlie later. "He thinks Avery's ride on her proves she'll flop with a new jockey. The Townsend kid's looking pretty cheerful, too."

Charlie shrugged. "Jennings is always doing a lot of talking. Most of it's hot air."

That weekend Jilly hobbled over to them as they were bringing Wonder back to her stall. She'd progressed from crutches to a cane, but she was far from ready to get in a saddle again.

"Craig just called me," she said. "He thinks he may have found a jock for you—Jimmy Hernandez. He's young, but Craig likes the way he rides."

Charlie loosened the chin strap on Wonder's bridle. "Matter of fact, Hernandez's agent called me last night, but I didn't know anything about the kid. Not the first agent to call me lately."

"You didn't tell me," Ashleigh said.

"No point. I've seen the others ride and don't like their style."

"Well, Craig thinks Hernandez might click. He's been winning a lot up in Arlington, and he's going to be coming down to ride at Keeneland anyway," Jilly said. "I know he's not nationally recognized yet—"

"Doesn't matter. The top jocks who aren't already committed seem to be shying away from her since Saratoga."

Ashleigh gave Charlie a look. The old trainer sure knew how to keep things to himself when he wanted.

"Hmph." Charlie frowned thoughtfully. "Suppose it's worth a shot. Let me talk to Townsend."

Ashleigh said nothing, but she felt a sick lump in her stomach. If Craig recommended Hernandez, he must be good. Her chances of riding were growing dimmer—and if Hernandez worked out . . . She decided she would take a chance and talk to Mr. Townsend now, before they contacted this new jock.

That afternoon she found him alone in his stable office. She'd carefully thought out what to say beforehand—how important it was for the farm for Wonder to do well; that Ashleigh had already proved that she could handle and get the most from Wonder; that she knew she was young and didn't have a license or experience in an actual race, but if this new jockey didn't work out, maybe they would consider her riding?

Mr. Townsend heard her out. But when she finished talking, he shook his head. "I know you can handle the filly and that she responds for you. That's not the problem. It's the physical risks involved. Just look at what happened to Jilly. I don't want to be responsible for someone your age getting injured. I can't see your parents agreeing, either. It's dangerous out there during a race. It's not the same as working a horse on the track. Every jock is set on winning—it can get fierce." He paused and stared at the wall, covered with photos of Townsend Acres' winning horses.

Wonder was there, draped in the blanket of roses after winning the Kentucky Derby. "There's nothing I'd like more than to see the Prince and Wonder challenge each other in the Breeder's Cup," Townsend said. "The two of them have been a financial godsend to the farm. The last couple of years, auction prices have been way down, and we haven't shown a profit on the breeding side of the operation. All of a sudden, we're getting a lot of interest again." He stopped and looked back at Ashleigh. "But I'm sorry, it's just not feasible. Charlie and Craig say we may have a shot with Hernandez. We'll have to go with that."

Ashleigh left his office with sagging shoulders. She hadn't really expected he'd say yes—that had just been her own little fantasy. But now the no was definite. Her balloon of hope had been popped.

They drove Wonder over to Keeneland several days before the Fayette. Charlie wanted the new jockey to have a chance to work the filly on the track there. Mike gave Ashleigh a lift to the track after school on Thursday.

"You look depressed," he said. "I probably shouldn't have suggested you talk to Townsend. His saying no only made you feel worse."

Ashleigh shook her head. "It's not your fault. I would have asked him anyway, I think."

"Well, wait and see how it goes," Mike said encouragingly. "This new jock may be okay."

Yet Charlie wouldn't say much about how the workout went. "Seems a nice kid," he said. "He's got gentle hands. I didn't give the filly a hard work. Just wanted the jock to get used to her. Best so far." He shrugged. "We'll see."

Terry wouldn't say much either. "She wasn't sizzling, but see how it goes on Saturday."

On Friday afternoon Mike flew up to join his father at Belmont for Jazzman's race in the Champagne. He was excited, but concerned about Wonder, too. "I'll keep my fingers crossed, and I'll call you Saturday night."

"Just do a good job with Jazzman," Ashleigh told him. "I'll be rooting for you."

That night Ashleigh walked up to Jilly's apartment to see what she thought.

"We've got to try to trust this guy," Jilly said. "But jeez, why can't I heal faster? There wouldn't be any problem if I could ride. Ash, I'm sorry."

"Why are you sorry?" Ashleigh asked. "It's not your fault. If anything, it's just the opposite."

Jilly looked down at her cast and cane. "Maybe, but I keep thinking back to that race, knowing she was wired. Maybe I could have done something more to quiet her."

"You couldn't have stopped that whip in her face."

"Yeah, true," Jilly admitted. "It's just such a bummer. She's come so far."

Ashleigh didn't have any answer to that.

Mr. Griffen drove Ashleigh and Linda over to Keeneland the next morning. Wonder knew a race was coming, since she hadn't been fed since breakfast. But when Jimmy Hernandez got in her saddle, she eyed Ashleigh, flicking her ears, whuffing uncertainly. It didn't seem to make any difference to Wonder that Hernandez had ridden her for two workouts. She was expecting Jilly's familiar hand and voice at race time.

"It's okay, girl," Ashleigh said. "Jimmy's going to give you a good ride. Just go out there and win it." She smiled up at the jockey, who smiled back. "I'll do my best," he promised.

"I hate to say it," Linda said with a sigh as she, Ashleigh, and Charlie headed toward the grandstand, "but she's not acting too happy. She doesn't have the fire like she usually does before a race."

"We've spoiled her rotten, haven't we, Charlie?" Ashleigh groaned. "No—I have! It's my fault. Other horses have different jockeys all the time and win. I've made her too much of a one-person horse!" Ashleigh slammed her fist against the wooden railing in frustration.

"Hold on, missy!" Charlie said sharply. "No one's to blame here, and I don't want to hear you getting down on yourself. Think of her early days, and remember she wouldn't be here now except for you. Maybe she needs a little special handling, but just look at what this filly's done. If special handling wins two parts of the Triple Crown, then I'm all for it. So let's not have any second thoughts about spoiling her or doing it different. We're here. We deal with the problem now."

It was a very long speech for Charlie. For a moment neither Ashleigh nor Linda said a word. Then Ashleigh spoke quietly. "Thanks, Charlie."

"It's the truth," he muttered.

Right up to the finish wire Ashleigh hoped that Hernandez would finally make that special connection with Wonder. But no such luck. Wonder never fired. Confused about her new rider, she broke slowly from the gate and got stuck behind other horses. She did rally somewhat, but in the stretch she didn't kick in. Ashleigh saw Hernandez automatically swing his hand for the whip he wasn't carrying, probably feeling frustration himself. They finished fourth behind horses Wonder should have beaten by lengths.

"No excuses," Hernandez said as he rode off the track. "One minute I felt like I had a lot of horse under me. The next minute, I didn't. She didn't click in the end."

Charlie just nodded. "Gave it your best."

That night Mike called as promised, and his news was wonderful. He could hardly talk, he was so excited. Jazzman had won and had run a very impressive race. "I wish you'd been here," he said ecstatically. "I couldn't believe it myself. He beat Archon by five lengths, and Brad's colt by six. I'm still barely breathing."

"You've got to enter him in the Breeder's Cup Juvenile," Ashleigh cried. "Archon's the top rated two-year-old this year. If you've already beaten him—"

"I can't," Mike said with a sudden note of sadness. "Jazzman wasn't nominated to the Breeder's Cup races. No one thought he'd do this well. And we can't afford the supplemental nomination fee. My dad and I talked it over. The fee's too much for us." His voice faded.

"Well," Ashleigh said sympathetically, "you still have the Derby next year, all the big three-year-old races."

Mike brightened a little. "Yeah, we're thinking of those. So tell me about Wonder's race."

Ashleigh did. Mike was silent for a moment when she'd finished. "You've got to ride her yourself. Forget what Townsend said. He might still change his mind."

"Maybe." But Ashleigh wasn't optimistic. "By the way, how did Townsend Prince do?"

"He won, easily. Sorry about that."

"I figured he would."

12

MR. TOWNSEND WAS WATCHING WHEN ASHLEIGH WORKED
Wonder a few days later at the farm. With Ashleigh
back in the saddle, the filly outdid herself, breaking
her own fast fractions for quarter-and-a-half-mile
works. Ashleigh was grinning from ear to ear as she
rode off the oval. She glanced at Mr. Townsend and
saw an expression of mixed bafflement and excitement on his face.

"She seems glad to have you back," Charlie said
with a twinkle as he held Wonder's head.

"She worked like a dream, Charlie!" Ashleigh said
as she jumped from the saddle. She patted the filly's
neck lovingly. "Didn't you, girl?"

Wonder snorted and bobbed her head. It didn't
take a horse expert to see that the filly was exhilarated
and a contented animal again.

"Wouldn't be surprised if Townsend thinks a little

141

more seriously about letting you ride," Charlie said quietly. "But let's not start counting our chicks too soon."

Ashleigh was afraid to get her hopes up. "He sounded pretty definite when he told me no."

"Things change," Charlie said.

As they headed back to the stable, Mr. Townsend joined them. "Charlie, I want your honest opinion. What are our chances in the Breeder's Cup Classic if Hernandez rides?"

"In my honest opinion, I doubt she'll click into the gear she'll need to beat the colts. Maybe she'd do better against the girls in the Distaff." Charlie lazily lifted his shaggy brows. "Then again, she might get used to Hernandez."

"I don't want to run her in the Distaff, and I don't want an indifferent performance."

"Then either take her out, or let Ashleigh ride," Charlie said bluntly. "The filly's had too tough a year. It's not worth messing her up when she's got at least another good year of racing ahead."

"Unfortunately, the farm needs the exposure *this* year."

Charlie shrugged. "Told you what I think."

Townsend tightened his mouth and stared thoughtfully into the distance. Ashleigh's heart had started racing at Charlie's suggestion. She felt close to fainting when Mr. Townsend turned to her. "You still want to ride?"

"Yes!"

"I've got to make the decision now to give you time to train. If your parents give their permission—and it'll have to be written—I'm willing to give it a shot. There's going to be a lot involved. You'll have to qualify for an apprentice license. I'll deal with all the paperwork, but before I let you go out in the Breeder's Cup, I want to see you get some experience on the track. Maddock has some seasoned mounts he'll be racing in the next couple of weeks. I'll talk to him and see what we can work out. I'll stop by and see your parents this afternoon, but if they say no—"

"I understand," Ashleigh gasped. "But I think they'll let me. It's so important."

"I hope they do. We'll see," Mr. Townsend said.

When he was gone, Ashleigh leaned against Wonder's shoulder. Her knees were shaking. She couldn't believe it. She felt like pinching herself.

Jilly had come up in time to hear this development. Now she reached out and hugged Ashleigh with her free arm. "Way to go! I knew he'd come around. And you can do it."

"You think so?"

"It's going to be a lot of work getting ready," Charlie said. "But I've never known you to back down from a challenge."

"No—I'm not going to back down! If you and Jilly think I can—"

"I'll put in a word to your parents," he said. "They're your biggest problem right now."

"Ashleigh, be reasonable," her father said sternly a few minutes later in his office. "We know you're a good rider, but you're not even sixteen. Riding in a race is dangerous, especially one as competitive as the Breeder's Cup. You could get hurt—easily. We're not about to risk that. I can't believe Townsend's even considering it."

"But, Dad, I'm going to be practicing. They're going to let me ride in a race beforehand. Jilly and Charlie think I can do it."

"Jilly and Charlie aren't your parents," Mrs. Griffen said. "I know they both care about you, but it's not the same. My heart would be in my throat with you out there in a race."

"You don't worry when I work Wonder, and I've ridden her at a real racetrack."

"Morning exercise is different from a serious race."

"But it's so important!" Ashleigh pleaded. "Wonder doesn't like any of the other jocks who've tried her, and she and I know each other."

"Yeah," Rory put in. He'd been listening to the whole argument. "You've got to let Ash ride. Wonder'd never hurt her!"

"I'm not worried about Wonder hurting her," Mrs. Griffen said. "I'm thinking of the dozen other horses that'll be in the field."

Charlie walked up behind them and cleared his throat. "Don't mean to butt in, but let me talk to your parents for a minute, missy."

Ashleigh took the cue. She motioned to Rory. "Let's go look at Lightning." Rory didn't want to leave, but at her frown he followed along. When they were out by the yearling paddock, Ashleigh leaned against the rail. She felt sick. Her parents had sounded so firm. She knew they weren't going to change their minds, even if Mr. Townsend talked to them.

"It would be so neat if you could ride in the Breeder's Cup," Rory said with a sigh.

"I know, Rory. It would be like a dream."

Ashleigh stayed clear of her parents until after she saw Mr. Townsend go down to their office. She was in agony, wondering what they were saying, praying Mr. Townsend could somehow convince them to let her ride. She thought about calling Linda and Mike, but what could they do? She'd wait until she knew one way or the other. Finally she wandered back up to the stables and hung around Wonder's stall, quietly grooming the filly, telling her how she felt.

A while later Charlie came down the aisle. "Thought you might be here. You might want to go down and see your parents. They've got some good news for you."

Ashleigh jumped up from where she'd been sitting on the tack box. "They said yes? Oh, my God. Really?"

Charlie gave one of his rare smiles. "Yup. We managed to convince them you're good enough. We're going to be busy."

"Thanks, Charlie! Thanks so much!"

"Don't thank me. Thank them."

The next few days were a whirlwind, but Ashleigh was walking on air and didn't mind the schedule Charlie and Jilly set out for her at all. She was going to ride Wonder in a race! Mike and Linda were almost as excited as she was.

"I told you so," Mike said when she told him. "You deserve it."

"You mean I'm going to be best friends with a star?" Linda teased.

"We might not win," Ashleigh reminded her.

"Oh, you will, Ash. I just know it!"

Around the farm stables, though, Ashleigh heard more negative than positive comments. Jim Jennings was one of the loudest critics, and when Brad came home from college for the weekend, he was furious.

Ashleigh heard him arguing with his father. "It's crazy. I can't believe you're letting her ride. She's never even ridden in a race!"

"It's a risk," his father agreed, "but we don't have any other options."

"There are plenty of jockeys who would take the ride. Stay with Hernandez."

"He can't get a good performance out of her."

"I don't know why you all baby that filly!" Brad stormed. "You bend over back—"

"Let's finish this conversation in my office," Mr. Townsend said with a touch of irritation. "And look at it from the business standpoint . . ."

Ashleigh heard no more, but she certainly felt Brad's snubs over the next days. And when he wasn't ignoring her, he was making snide, hurtful comments. The worst came when Ashleigh was out on the oval practicing, with Jilly and Charlie at the rail giving her instructions and advice. She heard Brad's remarks to the other riders when she rode off: "Lucky if she doesn't fall off at the gate," he sneered. "Can you see her trying to fight her way through a pack? No one's going to be holding her hand out there."

You think you could do better? Ashleigh thought. But she didn't dare say anything. She'd prove Brad wrong —she'd prove all the doubters wrong.

Each night she was exhausted and literally fell into

bed after finishing her homework. But she was getting plenty of moral support—Mike and Linda, Jilly and Charlie all believed in her. And now that her parents had made the decision to let her ride, they were behind her, too. When Caro came home for the weekend, she was thrilled with Ashleigh's news.

"Brad's absolutely livid—and being a complete snot," Ashleigh told her.

"What do you expect?" Caro laughed. "He knows Wonder can beat the Prince with you riding. He's probably scared out of his mind!"

Her friends at school thought Ashleigh's news was amazing. "Now we can really put on an incredible dance," Corey said. "We were going to use the Breeder's Cup theme anyway. The juniors and seniors can't look down their noses at us now."

Jennifer was the only one who was slightly miffed. Ashleigh was suddenly getting altogether too much attention. Not only was she with Mike all the time, but some of the older boys were stopping her in the hall to talk to her. Since they were usually only asking her how she felt about riding in the Breeder's Cup, Ashleigh didn't think much of it, but Jennifer did.

Charlie had Ashleigh break from the starting gate with other riders to get her used to horses running inside and outside of her. Ken Maddock, at Mr. Townsend's instructions, had assigned her a mount to ride in a small allowance race—if, of course, she passed the test for the track stewards to get her apprentice license.

Ashleigh was a nervous wreck the Sunday morning that Mr. Townsend, she, and Charlie drove to Keeneland so she could ride for the stewards. Ashleigh would ride the horse she'd been assigned in the race, a four-year-old colt who'd had plenty of experience racing. She had already ridden him at the farm and knew his quirks, but her hands felt clammy as she got in the saddle and picked up the reins.

"You'll do fine, missy," Charlie said. "Just relax."

She tried to as she went into the gate and waited for the bell and the doors to fly open. *I've done this at the farm*, she told herself. *I can do it now.* And she did. The gate opened, and she had the colt off in a shot. With the stewards watching, she galloped him, proved she had the skill to stay in the saddle and keep the horse going, then slow him down and stop him when she had to. Still, she rode off the track with a knot in her stomach.

Then she saw Mr. Townsend walk over with a smile and nod to Charlie. Charlie took the horse's reins. "All set."

Ashleigh let out a huge breath. "I passed?"

"You did," Mr. Townsend answered. "You'll be riding in the sixth race Wednesday. Congratulations!"

"We played down your age," Charlie told her. "It'll

be all over the papers before the Breeder's Cup, but no point advertising it now."

Ashleigh left school at noon the day of the race. Mr. Townsend, Charlie, and Jilly picked her up. She was so thankful for Jilly's company. Jilly knew exactly what it was like to ride in your first race—and as a female. The older girl went with Ashleigh to the jockeys' quarters when Ashleigh changed, and introduced her around. Maybe because Jilly was there like a protective shadow, none of the other riders made any comments and accepted her explanation that she'd been exercise riding regularly at Townsend Acres. She didn't mention Wonder, and fortunately no one made the connection between her and the filly. They didn't seem to be suspicious about her age either, perhaps because all jockeys were small and tended to look younger than they were.

Jilly stood to the side as Ashleigh, dressed in her green and gold Townsend Acres silks, weighed in with her saddle. Then Charlie and Mr. Townsend joined them as they went out to the saddling area.

Ashleigh was so nervous she couldn't think straight, but the others were calm and businesslike, and that helped clear the cotton from her brain. Ken Maddock gave her some last-minute instructions.

"We're lucky. It's going to be a small field. You shouldn't have any problems with getting blocked or bounced around too much. Hawking will want to run near the lead, so get him out fast. Wake him up as you're coming off the backstretch. He shouldn't need much—just show him the crop. We're not necessarily expecting to win, but he should come in second or third without any trouble."

"Good luck," they all said as Ashleigh got a leg up into the saddle.

Ashleigh glanced at the other jockeys, all experienced riders. They seemed so calm. She wasn't. She took a deep, steadying breath, but soon she had other things to think about besides her nervousness—the crowds in the stand, the post parade, the warm-up jog, and the state of the horse beneath her. The race was a six-furlong sprint. The gate was positioned in the chute at the head of the backstretch. They'd race down the backstretch, around the far turn, and under the wire in front of the grandstand.

They loaded third. Hawking was an old pro and went in and stood quietly. Ashleigh readied herself, positioned her hands on the reins, and gripped a chunk of Hawking's mane. Then she looked straight ahead between the colt's ears, waiting for the bell and the opening gate. *Do this right!* she told herself.

She was ready when the doors flipped open, and instantly urged Hawking forward. Hawking needed to get clear of the horses to either side of him before the end of the chute. Ashleigh clucked to Hawking and slid her hands forward along his neck. He responded and pulled them forward. One horse had taken the lead along the rail, and Ashleigh angled over to settle in a half-length behind, ready to challenge the lead when they reached the end of the backstretch. Never had the backstretch seemed so long in her workouts. Never had she been so aware of the pounding thud of hooves and snorted breaths of the horses around her. She thought of nothing now but having Hawking ready at the turn. She sensed a horse coming up on her outside and knew she couldn't wait much longer. The turn loomed ahead.

They swept into it. She clucked to Hawking, gave him rein. "Let's go!" The colt's ears were back, listening, but he didn't accelerate as she'd expected! Suddenly she remembered the whip in her hand. She never used one with Wonder, but she remembered Maddock's instructions. She waved it quickly by the colt's eye, and with that, he dug in. But she'd lost valuable seconds! The horse inside was still in the lead and fighting. She clucked to Hawking again, flicked the crop, and kneaded her hands along his neck the way she always did with Wonder. He wasn't a horse of Wonder's caliber, but he was trying. Slowly they moved up on the front horse. *Another few strides, and we'll have him!* Ashleigh thought. But there wasn't room. The one horse went under the wire with his nose in front.

Ashleigh stood in the stirrups and patted Hawking's neck. "You did your best. You gave it a good try." But what would Mr. Townsend and Ken Maddock have to say? Had her hesitation with the whip lost them the race? As she rode off the track, she looked anxiously at their faces.

But Maddock walked up to her with a smile. "Nice effort. He did better than I thought."

Ashleigh expelled the breath she'd been holding. "I rode okay then?"

"You did everything just fine," Mr. Townsend told her. "The Classic's going to be a much tougher race, but I feel a lot better about you riding after what I saw today."

13

"I'M SURPRISED THEY'RE NOT SAYING ANYTHING ABOUT YOU RID-ing," Linda remarked, looking up from the sports pages and racing papers spread over the floor of Jilly's apartment.

"Mr. Townsend and Charlie are keeping it quiet until the race."

"How's Brad been acting?" Mike asked.

Jilly handed around cold sodas and broke open a bag of popcorn. "Like a jerk. He sure doesn't want Ashleigh to ride. He's still trying to convince his father to put up a 'real' jock—his words. Thank heavens he's only here on weekends."

"And the Prince has already gone to Louisville," Ashleigh said. "Wonder goes Wednesday. Charlie wanted to keep her here as long as possible, so I could work her."

"From what I saw this morning," Linda put in, "she's ready."

"Yeah, she's ready." Ashleigh bit her lip. "I just hope I am."

"You are," Jilly said firmly. "You wouldn't be normal if you weren't getting nervous. I was a basket case before the Derby!"

That was reassuring to hear, but Ashleigh could barely think straight by Thursday afternoon. Her friends crowded around her at lunch and after school, wishing her well, telling her it didn't matter if she won—it was just so incredible that she was actually riding in as important a race as the Classic.

On Thursday night the Griffens drove Ashleigh and Jilly to Louisville. Charlie was already at the track, and Linda would be there, too, helping her father get his horse ready for the turf race. Mike would be driving over on Friday afternoon. If Ashleigh hadn't felt so tense, the weekend would have seemed like one big party. The activity at Churchill Downs was as intense as Derby week.

Charlie had Ashleigh work Wonder over the track the next morning, and Linda and Jilly both came to watch. The word was out that Ashleigh would be riding in the race, and the backside was buzzing with talk.

Ashleigh was very aware of the interested stares as she moved Wonder out. Wonder moved like a charged ball of energy, and Ashleigh had to keep her firmly in hand. But at the end of the work, Ashleigh felt satisfied, and Wonder was tossing her elegant head, knowing she'd done well.

Craig Avery was standing with the others as Ashleigh rode off the track. "She looked good," he said. "She's ready to roll. I'm glad you're getting the chance to ride. And don't listen to any of the talk."

"What talk?" Ashleigh asked.

Charlie understood and frowned. "The other jocks planning on giving her a hard time?"

"I wouldn't go that far," Craig answered. "But they're not going to make it easy. They think she's too green a rider and won't be able to work herself out of a pinch." He turned to Ashleigh. "They're not going to be out there helping you, that's for sure. Be prepared. Stay on top of things every second."

"You think she should trust you?" Jilly grinned. "You'll be out there riding against her on the Prince."

"I ride a clean race," Craig answered indignantly, but he knew Jilly was teasing.

Several reporters followed them as they headed back to the barn, hammering both Charlie and Ashleigh with questions. Ashleigh was still mulling over what Craig had said, and she didn't want to answer questions anyway, afraid she'd say too much.

"Leave her alone," Charlie finally barked. "You'll get your answers tomorrow."

"You ever find out what happened at Saratoga?" one persistent reporter called. "You afraid she's going to come unglued again?"

"Nope. I'm not." Charlie refused to say more, and the reporters gave up and went out in search of more cooperative prey.

"Whew!" Linda said as they left. "They're not going to give you much peace, are they?"

"Goes with the territory," Charlie muttered.

Mr. Townsend came by the stall later in the morning. Ashleigh had seen Brad moving around the barn, putting up a smiling and confident front for the reporters. But he didn't look very confident when they weren't around. He was sullen and his mouth was tight. His father seemed frankly worried as he talked to Charlie. Ashleigh couldn't hear what they were saying, but she wondered if he was questioning his decision to let her ride. She didn't even dare ask Charlie afterward.

Just before dinner Mike arrived, and Ashleigh hurried to meet him as he walked up to the stall. She felt more relaxed just seeing his smiling face, and she desperately needed to talk to him. He had become very important to her, so gradually that she only noticed it now with surprise. Linda and her father had gone out with the owner of their horse. Jilly was with Craig, and Charlie was off chatting with some other trainers.

She was feeling very alone with her worries for the next day's race.

Mike greeted Wonder, then sat down on the tack box next to Ashleigh. "So how're you feeling?" he asked.

"Nervous," said Ashleigh, looking worriedly into his eyes.

He took her hand and squeezed it. "I don't blame you. But you know you're a good enough rider, and with you in the saddle, the filly's going to run her heart out."

"If nothing wrong happens at the gate, and we don't get blocked in."

"You've got to be prepared, but try thinking of the good things, too. Wonder will try to pull you straight to the front, and once you're there, you should be clear of trouble. It's not like she's a late closer."

"Craig told me to be prepared, too." She went on to tell him what the other jockey had said, then filled him in on all the news and gossip on the backside. As they talked, Charlie strolled up.

He nodded a greeting to Mike. "So you got here. Traffic's pretty bad, I guess."

"Crazy."

Ashleigh noticed that Charlie was looking grimmer than usual. He was scowling and seemed to have something on his mind. She also noticed him and Mike exchange a private look.

"What's wrong?" she asked.

"Nothing's wrong," the trainer said. "You've been sitting here all afternoon. Time you took a break. You're looking chilled."

Ashleigh hadn't realized she'd been rubbing her arms. In the evening air her sweatshirt wasn't enough, and she'd forgotten to bring her jacket.

"Go get into something warmer," Charlie said. "And on your way back, you can stop in the kitchen and pick up some sandwiches, coffee for me, and whatever you're drinking." He dug in his pocket and handed her some crumpled bills.

Ashleigh didn't want to leave now that Mike was there, but she wasn't about to argue with Charlie. And she did need warmer clothes. She took the money, found out what kind of sandwiches Charlie and Mike wanted, and set off. Strangely, Mike and Charlie almost looked relieved to see her go. It had to be her imagination. They were probably both starving.

It took her longer than she'd expected to get her jacket and the food. The track kitchen was crowded, and she had to wait in a long line. With laden arms, she finally walked through the now-quiet backside to the Townsend barn.

The area around Wonder's stall wasn't quiet, though. A crowd was gathering, and in its midst she saw Mike and Charlie. Something was wrong with

Wonder! She rushed forward, dropping the sand-wiches on a bench before she pushed through to Mike and Charlie. She stopped and stared again. They each held the arm of a young groom, who looked terrified.

"What's going on?" Ashleigh cried.

Charlie and Mike didn't seem to hear her, there was so much commotion. Two track officials strode over just then, and Ashleigh listened in a daze as they talked to Charlie.

"We caught him red-handed, trying to spook the filly," Charlie said. "I've had my suspicions since the Travers—started me thinking back to the way she was before the Belmont. Didn't seem like coincidence to me. The filly was being spooked deliberately."

Only then did Ashleigh notice the crop the groom held in hand.

"Glad you told us to hang around," one official said.

"Figured we had to set it up and leave the filly unguarded, if we were going to catch him," Charlie said. "And if anything was going to happen, it had to be tonight."

The groom had grown paler by the second. When the official swung toward him, he turned paper white. "Who put you up to it?"

"Nobody. I wasn't doing nothing . . . just stand-ing here."

"With a crop, swinging it at the filly. We've got

eye-witnesses. You might as well come clean. You're not doing yourself any good."

"I'm not saying nothing," he said sullenly.

"Fine—you can take the whole rap. The owner will be pressing charges. You can think about it in jail."

The groom obviously hadn't thought of that before. He looked around for the help that wasn't there, then broke down into a snarl. "I needed the money! He said there wasn't any way I'd get caught!"

"Who said?"

"Jennings."

"Jim Jennings?" Charlie cried. "The assistant trainer at Townsend Acres?"

"That's him. I knew him from when he ran horses here," the groom babbled. "He came by a couple of days ago. Waved a wad of money in my face. Said there'd be more if the filly lost the race, and told me what to do."

"But why?" Ashleigh gasped.

"How would I know?" the groom grumbled. "I just did what he said."

Charlie's mouth was tight with anger. "Don't suppose you know anything about what happened at Saratoga? A jock got hurt, could have been killed!"

"Not me! I've never been there! I only work this track."

"Come along with us," one of the officials said. "Townsend's on his way," he added to Charlie. "We

161

reached him at his hotel. The police have been noti-
fied, too. Nice work. You may have prevented a trag-
edy."

The officials took the groom and led him off. The
crowd started buzzing. "Can't believe it . . . one of
Townsend's own trainers . . . guy's gotta be nuts
. . . must be drugs involved . . . what put you on
to it, Charlie?"

As Charlie answered questions, Ashleigh went over
to Mike, looking behind him to Wonder's stall. She
was having trouble taking it all in.

"We stopped him before the filly got too upset,"
Mike said. "She'll probably be better for seeing you,
though."

Ashleigh was already on her way to the stall, with
Mike right behind her. Wonder was standing in the
shadows near the back, quivering, but she saw Ashleigh and immediately nickered. Ashleigh went into
the stall. "Yeah, girl, easy," she murmured, rubbing
Wonder's neck soothingly. "I don't blame you for being upset. We're just lucky Mike and Charlie caught
him." Wonder touched her nose to Ashleigh's shoulder and huffed her distress.

"How could he do that to her?" Ashleigh said to
Mike. "And I still don't understand why. Does he
hate her being a success that much?"

"I think there's probably more to it than that."

"Jennings has always given me the creeps, but I

didn't think he was that rotten. You don't think . . . no, maybe I shouldn't think it either."

"What? That Brad was behind it?" Mike asked.

Ashleigh looked up at him. "You were thinking the same thing, too?"

"Charlie and I considered it."

"Why didn't you tell me what you were planning?" Ashleigh felt hurt at being left in the dark.

"I wanted to. Charlie said you'd have enough on your mind, riding in the Classic. He was right."

"But you had it all worked out. You sent me off deliberately. When did you plan all this? Why did Charlie think something would happen?"

"He said something to me after the Travers. He'd started making connections—the filly only got wired just before the Belmont, then settled right back down again at the farm. After the Fayette, he was pretty sure someone was deliberately spooking her."

"I don't understand. She was calm before that race."

"That's it. With a strange jockey in the saddle, no one thought she would win anyway—at least those who knew her. But when Townsend decided to let you ride her in the Classic, Charlie started getting worried. He asked me if I'd help him tonight. He figured if it was deliberate, they'd move when the backside was at its quietest—dinnertime. We made a show of walking off, talking about getting something to eat, but we circled back and hid where we could watch the stall. It was just about dark. The groom must have been waiting for his chance. He walked up to the stall a few minutes later, looking around. The filly was standing by the door. When he saw the coast was clear, he lifted the crop and started swinging it in front of her face. Charlie and I moved in. If nothing had happened now, we were going to keep an all-night guard on the stall."

"It's just so incredible that Jennings would do this," Ashleigh said with a sigh.

Wonder was a little better as they left the stall. "We'll be right outside, girl," Ashleigh said. "No one's going to bother you again."

Wonder whuffed, but flicked her ears nervously at the voices beyond the stall. The crowd had thinned, although the news must have spread because there were plenty of stable hands back in the barn, and Ashleigh saw people mulling between the barn buildings. Track guards kept them away.

Charlie had found the bags of food Ashleigh had dropped on the bench and carried them over. "Might as well keep our strength up. Coffee will be cold by now, though." He pulled over a folding chair.

"Charlie, you're great to have figured all this out," Ashleigh said.

"There are some advantages to being old," he muttered. "You've seen enough to know when something's not right. Townsend's on his way over, by the way. He sent someone up to surprise Jennings at the farm. Should be interesting to hear what he has to say."

Not long after, Mr. Townsend showed up in person, in a suit and tie, dressed for dinner. "Charlie, I don't know what to say." He found another folding chair and sat down. "The police talked to Jennings at the farm. Maddock is on his way over. From what they've found out so far, Jennings is our man, all right. Looks like he's over his head in gambling debt, borrowed from the wrong people. To get himself off the hook, he agreed to help fix a few races—spook the filly so she'd lose, and of course, he knew how. How is she?"

"She was upset," Ashleigh answered. "But she should relax if we keep her quiet."

"I don't know how I could have been so blind about his character," Townsend said. "Needless to say, he's fired—if he doesn't end up in jail."

There was still plenty of talk in the barn the following morning, but with Mike and Charlie standing guard, no one got within yards of Wonder's stall. Ashleigh and Mike took her out for a morning walk. Charlie was afraid that even light exercise on the

165

track would overexcite her again. Linda joined them, looking hyper.

"I just heard what happened last night!" she gasped, trying to keep her voice low for Wonder's benefit. "I don't believe it—but it explains a lot, doesn't it?"

"It sure does," Ashleigh said.

"She looks okay, though," Linda added, giving the filly a careful scrutiny.

"Mike and Charlie stopped him before she got too wired." Ashleigh didn't want to talk about the incident the night before. It made her think of the race ahead, and that made her stomach knot. "How's everything going at your barn?"

Linda ran a hand through her blond curls. "Good. Daysailer's fine. We're certainly not going in as the favorite, but Dad's feeling fairly confident. Heck, just to place would be something in this kind of competition." She studied Ashleigh's face. "How're you feeling?"

"Great—if I don't think about this afternoon."

"You'll have all of us as a pep club," Linda said. "Just think of all those good vibrations. I came by the Prince's stall on my way here. Brad's really holding court."

"So what's surprising about that?"

"I just thought after last night, maybe he'd be a little upset."

"Wait till you see him without the crowd around him," Mike told her. "He's upset all right—and worried, too."

Ashleigh frowned. "Do you think he knew what was going on?"

"I think he guessed."

When Mike and Ashleigh brought Wonder back to the stall, Charlie was talking to Jerry Barns of *The Daily Racing Form*. He was the only reporter Charlie had allowed near him. Barns smiled at Ashleigh, but Wonder snorted nervously at the sight of a stranger.

"She still shook up?" he asked Charlie.

"She's settling. I wouldn't worry about it."

"Last night sure put the press in a tailspin," Barns said. "That, and the fact that you're riding." He grinned at Ashleigh. "There are a lot of skeptics out there. I'd say the filly will go in at about fourth betting choice."

"That doesn't bother us," Charlie said.

"I didn't think it would. Good luck. Personally I'm hoping that guts and heart win the day. I've already got that column written."

The next hours were so hectic that Ashleigh didn't have time to think. Terry Bush groomed Wonder, but Ashleigh spent as much time as she could in or near the stall. Her parents, Rory, Caroline, and Justin arrived around noon. Rory was so excited, he could barely talk, but her parents were more apprehensive.

"I'm not sure if I'm ready for this," Mrs. Griffen said as she hugged Ashleigh. "I'm a wreck."

"Elaine, we made the decision, and Ashleigh's got enough on her mind."

Mrs. Griffen nodded distractedly at her husband. "Oh, I know. And I am behind you, Ashleigh. Please, just be *careful*."

Ashleigh returned her mother's hug. "I will, Mom. I know you're worried, but Wonder and I will be okay. She's not going to let me down."

Her father gave her a squeeze and a kiss. "I think we'll do more good out in the grandstand. There's enough commotion around here. We'll be rooting for you, sweetheart. Good luck."

"Thanks, Dad."

"Don't worry about Mom," Caro whispered as she gave Ashleigh her own good-luck hug. "She was fine till we got here and someone reminded her of Jilly's accident."

"That's not going to happen today," Ashleigh said. But she'd been thinking about it, too.

14

THE AFTERNOON SEEMED TO DRAG AFTER THAT. THERE WAS LIT-
tle more Ashleigh could do to keep busy after the
seven-race program began. No matter where she went
on the track, the excitement was heady and intense,
and a reminder of what was ahead. At least Mike and
Jilly were there with her, and Jilly would go with her
to the jockeys' quarters when it was time to change.
Linda was busy with their horse, and Ashleigh
guessed she was a wreck, too. Daysailer was running
in the fourth race, the Turf Mile, and she wouldn't
expect to see much of Linda until afterwards.

Ashleigh was reluctant to leave Wonder, but Charlie wanted her to have a firsthand look at how the
track was handling. Mike and Terry stood guard at
the stall, while Charlie, Jilly, and Ashleigh went out to
watch the third race, the Distaff. It was the race Wonder would have been entered in, if Mr. Townsend

hadn't decided he wanted Wonder to run against Townsend Prince. The race was a mile and an eighth. Wonder would be competing at a mile and a quarter.

As Ashleigh watched, she had the certain feeling that Wonder could have tromped the field and been an easy victor. Charade went under the wire a half-length in front to win the Distaff. Craig was riding the winner, and Jilly gave a whoop, but Ashleigh was remembering that Wonder had beaten Charade by lengths the year before.

The Turf Mile was next on the card, and since Daysailer was running, they went to the paddock area and waited until the horses were brought in to be saddled. Ashleigh saw Linda and her father arrive and gave her friend the high sign.

"What do you think of Daysailer?" Ashleigh asked Charlie when the saddled horses were led out into the walking ring.

"Got a nice look to him," Charlie said. "But I'd have to know more about him before I could make any judgments. From his record in the form, he looks like he's coming along."

The mile would be run on the inner, turf course. Ashleigh crossed her fingers as they went to watch, hoping Linda would have something to cheer about. And in the end the Marches did! Daysailer made a late drive and finished a closing second in the field of twelve. Linda and her father would be overjoyed.

With each of the following races, Ashleigh's anxiety grew. The Classic was the seventh and last race and wouldn't go off until after five. Wonder had started to pace her stall and fidget, which didn't make Ashleigh feel any better, although the filly wasn't nearly as high-strung as she'd been before the Belmont and Travers. Charlie sat down with Ashleigh and went over his strategy—get out near the front, lay in striking distance, and try to stay clear of pockets even if it meant running wide.

At last Jilly motioned to Ashleigh. "Let's go. Give you something to do besides chew on your nails." As before, Jilly smoothed the way with the other jockeys. Now, though, Ashleigh received a lot of quizzical, probing glances. She noticed a few doubtful head shakes, too. Jilly kept up a steady chatter to keep Ashleigh's mind occupied, and Craig gave Ashleigh a smile and a wink from across the room. Both of them wore the green-and-gold Townsend silks.

"You're going to have trouble knowing who to cheer for," Ashleigh said to Jilly.

"It's no contest. Craig's already won two races today. He knows where my heart lies in this one."

Mike, Charlie, and Terry were waiting in the saddling area when Ashleigh and Jilly walked up.

"You look great," Mike whispered to Ashleigh as Charlie took the saddle from her. "Like a real pro."

"Thanks," she said, smiling weakly. "I wish I felt like a pro."

Wonder was tacked and ready to go. Charlie gave Terry the signal to lead her out to the walking ring. Ashleigh felt strange, watching from the sidelines; stranger still when she looked down and saw gleaming, feather-light boots and shining silks on herself. She rubbed her hands together. They were already starting to sweat. Mike took one of them and squeezed it. "You'll be okay. Relax. You're a darned good rider."

Ashleigh swallowed and nodded, then gazed out to study the other horses in the field. Townsend Prince looked cool and collected and completely alert. Two of the other big horses in the field, Mercy Man and Excalibur, were impressive, too. Mercy Man danced on slender black legs. Excalibur threw up his head and eyed the crowd, and drew attention for his elegant appearance alone. Then there were the older horses, who would really present a challenge. Wonder was on her toes, occasionally snatching at her lead. As the only filly in the field, and such a well-known one, she was getting her own share of attention from the crowd.

Ashleigh saw Mr. Townsend approaching. His eyes were on Wonder as Terry walked her. "She looks okay," he said to Charlie. "I only hope I haven't made a mistake running her in the Classic. If it looks like the race is going to be too hard on her, Ashleigh, don't push her. This challenge between her and the Prince isn't worth ruining her."

He strode off, and Charlie lifted his hat and scratched his head. "Now what was that all about?"

"Maybe Brad's been getting through to him," Jilly said. "He never wanted Wonder to run in the Classic, let alone have Ashleigh ride."

Charlie pursed his lips. "Could be, too, he's feeling a little rattled after last night. This filly's worth a lot of money to him."

Ashleigh felt uneasy. "Do you think it's going to be too much of a strain on her?" she asked Charlie.

"I would have preferred the Distaff, but I would have put her out of commission myself if I thought this race would ruin her. She's already beaten three-quarters of the colts in this field. It's the older horses we might have to worry about. No, you just judge for yourself. You know the filly inside and out. She'll tell you if she's had enough."

It was time for the jockeys to mount. Jilly squeezed Ashleigh around the shoulders. "Stay cool. If I can do it, you can do it."

Mike gave her a beaming smile and a quick kiss on the cheek—even though everyone was watching. "I'll just say the lucky words—see you in the winner's circle. Good luck."

Ashleigh returned the warm pressure of his fingers

on her hand, took a deep breath, straightened her shoulders, and walked out to the ring. She saw Linda and Mr. March's faces in the crowd on the other side. Linda was grinning from ear to ear and mouthed the words, "Go get 'em!"

Ashleigh fastened the chin strap on her helmet, and Charlie gave her a leg up into the saddle. Wonder suddenly craned her head around and nickered gleefully.

"She's glad to see you up there," Charlie chuckled. "Matter of fact, I don't think she believes it. I've got faith in the two of you, missy," he added almost under his breath. "Win or lose, you'll do this old man proud." Charlie immediately pulled down the brim of his hat. He wasn't one for sentimentality, so his mumbled words meant all the more.

He walked with them as they circled the ring again. Now Ashleigh noticed the looks directed at the old trainer, the cameras aimed in his direction. He hadn't been forgotten, even if Wonder was the first horse he'd trained after six years of forced retirement.

When it was time to go out under the grandstand to the track, Charlie patted Wonder's shoulder and squinted up at Ashleigh. "You just remember what I told you beforehand, and let the filly do the rest. You'll do fine."

He left them as Terry led them through the tunnel

to the waiting escort ponies. Terry wished her a smiling good luck, too, as the exercise rider took control of Wonder and led them on.

Ashleigh was on her own. Ahead was the track, to either side were tiers of seats filled with cheering spectators. For a paralyzing instant, she was consumed by panic. She couldn't think; she couldn't move; she couldn't breathe. Then Wonder snorted and tossed her head, pulling the reins against Ashleigh's hands, and Ashleigh realized she *wasn't* alone. She and her precious filly were in this together. And they'd do their best—together. Just as she'd always dreamed—from the first moment she had seen Wonder as a sickly, too-small foal three years earlier.

"I'm here, girl," she whispered. Wonder flicked back her perfectly shaped ears, listening. "I know we can do it, don't you?"

Wonder whuffed and arched her muscled neck. She picked up her feet with more spring. *She knows*, Ashleigh thought. *She understands. I love you, Wonder. No matter what.*

The pony rider turned back and smiled. "Nice filly," she said. "You guys make a good pair. My money's on you."

As they cantered in line with the rest of the field, Ashleigh was sure Wonder did understand that the two of them had something special to do that day.

Ashleigh could feel the elated tension in the horse beneath her—Wonder's eagerness and fitness—and most of all, her desire to win. They were communicating with each other. Never had Ashleigh felt so in tune with the filly. It was as if they were reading each other's minds.

They came up to the gate. Charlie had seen their Number Two post position as a disadvantage. If Ashleigh didn't get Wonder out fast enough, horses outside of them would swing in toward the rail and block them. They'd all be fighting to save ground along the inside.

Ashleigh clucked to Wonder when it came their turn to load, and Wonder walked in like a lady. A gate attendant clung to the partition to their left, there to steady Wonder if she misbehaved. Another jumped up on the partition to their right as the three horse loaded. Ashleigh ran a hand over Wonder's neck while the other nine horses loaded. She saw the last few going in and settled herself, gripping the reins and a bit of Wonder's long and silky mane. She looked straight ahead between Wonder's alert ears and waited, every muscle tense. Horses snorted to either side of her. Jockeys and attendants made quick, terse remarks. Jilly's accident flashed before Ashleigh's eyes in slow motion, but she couldn't think of that. Instead, she visualized her and Wonder going under the wire in front. Simultaneously bells rang and gate doors flipped open. Ashleigh heeled Wonder and yelled, "Go!"

They burst from the gate with one powerful thrust of Wonder's hindquarters. In strides, they were clear of the worst of the pack. Ashleigh didn't even have time to be thankful. Everything was concentrated ahead. They eased into third, just off the pace, although Ashleigh didn't forget for an instant that there were nine powerful Thoroughbreds pounding behind them, breathing down their necks. She knew, too, that things wouldn't really start happening until the far turn, when everyone would be fighting for position for the stretch. She kept Wonder steady around the clubhouse turn and into the backstretch. The filly seemed to be pacing herself, knowing exactly what she should do, reserving her strength for the last rush, when it would be so necessary. The field today wasn't going to make it easy. From the corner of her eye, Ashleigh saw a horse moving up on their outside. In a moment Wonder saw it, too, and started trying to pull them forward on her own. Ashleigh made a flash decision and let Wonder out a notch—praying she wasn't letting the filly use up too much speed.

They were in second now and approaching the far turn. It was from here on out that things would get critical. The horse inside of them, Foregone, was a well-reputed four-year-old who had the ability to go wire to wire. Ashleigh was more concerned about the horses that would be ranging up quickly outside of her—the Prince, Excalibur, and Mercy Man. It flashed through Ashleigh's mind that the race was going too easily, that she'd expected more jostling and fighting than this.

A second later she regretted her thoughts. They were into the far turn, and suddenly everything was happening! Foregone accelerated along the rail. A horse was roaring up on her outside. One sidewise glance told her it was Excalibur, and outside of him she recognized the jockey's silks of Townsend Prince.

"Good-bye, baby!" the jockey on Excalibur called as he zoomed up past Wonder.

She'd waited too long! Excalibur angled over in front of her. Townsend Prince was on his outside. Foregone was holding firm on the inside—three of them nose and nose—with Wonder suddenly blocked behind them. Another horse had moved up outside of Wonder. Wonder's nose was practically between the flanks of the horses in front, and there wasn't room to angle out! Wonder was showing her distress at being blocked—she was ready to climb over the horses in front. Ashleigh was forced to check the filly.

I've lost it! she thought in panic. *I am too green. I should have been prepared!*

Then she spotted the narrowest of openings on the rail. It would be tight . . . maybe too tight. Wonder might not be willing to go through, but it was the only chance they had.

Ashleigh glanced behind to her left, saw no one blocking her there. She turned the filly's head toward the rail. Wonder saw the opening, and moved. In one stride, she angled, in the next, she was in the slot, in the next, she was pushing through courageously. They were only a fraction of an inch off the rail, nearly brushing it, but Wonder had seen her chance and wasn't about to let anything stop her.

"That's the way, girl!" Ashleigh gasped. "Let's get 'em!"

Now there were four of them across the track as they came into the stretch. Wonder's mane whipped in Ashleigh's face as Ashleigh crouched low over the filly's neck. At the merest signal from Ashleigh, Wonder changed leads. And with the change came a new burst of speed. Ashleigh could feel the power and strength still left in the filly, and it was heady! Foregone started dropping back, but Excalibur and Townsend Prince were running strong, not about to give up the battle. Ashleigh finally gave Wonder all the rein she wanted, kneaded her hands along the filly's neck, and clucked in Wonder's ear—signals they both knew well. She felt the filly dig in and drive forward. "Let's win it!" Ashleigh cried. "Go, baby!"

At the eighth pole Ashleigh glanced to the right. She saw noses. At the sixteenth pole, she saw nothing, but she wasn't about to ease up yet—and neither was Wonder. Just before the wire, she looked right again, then behind, to see Excalibur and Townsend Prince eating her dust. She felt a surge of incredible joy. She knew they'd done it. They were going to win!

Then they were under the wire. Ashleigh stood in her stirrups and raised her arm victoriously in the air. "We did it, Wonder! We won the Classic!" she cried. The filly knew. She tossed her elegant head as they turned and cantered back down the track to see the rest of the field cantering toward them. A second later Craig rode Townsend Prince alongside.

"Congratulations!" he grinned. "Told you you could do it."

Ashleigh was breathless. She was so excited and choked with emotion that she could barely talk. "Thanks!"

"I thought we had you coming off the turn. Then I glance over and see you shooting through on the rail. We held on for a second, but we only beat Excalibur by the hair on the Prince's nose. Darned good ride. I'll have to watch the replays to see exactly how you did it."

"It wasn't just me." Ashleigh laughed. "Wonder had more to do with it than I did." She'd never been so happy in her whole life. She kept patting Wonder's neck and cooing praise in Wonder's ears, but as Craig cantered ahead, she realized she could barely see for the happy tears in her eyes. She wouldn't be able to find the winner's circle at this rate. Fortunately, the same escort rider who'd led them in came to lead them out. "Hey, hey," she laughed as she took Wonder's reins and led them off. "I knew I was right about you guys. You're going to get some reception in the winner's circle!"

The next minutes would always seem a happy blur to Ashleigh. The cheering crowds, the cameras, Charlie's beaming face as he held Wonder while Ashleigh dismounted, took the saddle and weighed in, then mounted again for more photos with the blanket of flowers draped over Wonder's shoulders; Wonder flinging up her head proudly and putting on a show for the spectators; the hugs and kisses from her family and friends, and Mike. "You don't have to cry," he smiled as he gently brushed a tear from her cheek.

"I'm just so happy!"

Terry draped Wonder in a green and gold satin sheet, and a euphoric Mr. Townsend led Charlie and Ashleigh to the white-railed presentation platform. There were more photos, and a television commentator holding a microphone, asking each of them for their reactions. Ashleigh wasn't even sure what she said.

Then the trophy was presented to Mr. Townsend. But after he accepted it, he added, "I have an announcement to make. As all of you probably know, if it wasn't for this young woman's efforts, Ashleigh's Wonder might never have made it here. We didn't have faith in the filly, but Ashleigh Griffen did. I think faith and courage like that deserve a reward. Today, Ashleigh, I'm turning over half ownership of Ashleigh's Wonder to you, with my deepest thanks for the contribution you've both made to Townsend Acres."

A hush had fallen over the crowd. Ashleigh stared at Mr. Townsend, aghast. Was she dreaming? Had she heard what she thought she heard? He was giving her half interest in Wonder?

Mr. Townsend smiled at her. "Having trouble taking it in?" he chuckled. "I mean every word of it. Congratulations."

Ashleigh took the hand he extended and stuttered her thanks. There was a wave of murmured pleasure from the crowd, then loud applause and cheers. Ashleigh stared numbly, first at Mr. Townsend, then at the other well-wishers. Her head was spinning, but gradually it began to sink in. Wonder was half hers! She would never have to be parted from the filly! She started to smile and couldn't stop even though her eyes were blurring with tears. Again, she thanked Mr. Townsend. From the corner of her eye, she saw Brad stalk off in a fury, but now microphones were thrust in her face. "This has been quite a day for you!" the commentator praised. "How are you feeling?"

"Like I'm dreaming!" Ashleigh laughed. "But it's wonderful!"

He turned to his cameras. "So there you have it, ladies and gentlemen, a history-making day in Thoroughbred racing in all respects. We'd like to add our congratulations to this courageous young lady and this gallant filly. May you both have many more successes."

At last the crowd thinned, the reporters drifted away. Ashleigh was trembling. It still seemed so hard to believe! She turned to Mr. Townsend and tried to thank him more coherently.

"As I said, Ashleigh, you deserve it. My only stipulation is that we keep the filly on the farm," he smiled.

"Of course! I—I'm not going anywhere."

"Not for the moment, maybe. The half interest in Wonder's winnings should give you a nice nest egg for college, and meanwhile, I wouldn't object to you and Charlie taking a hand in the training of some of the other horses on the farm. We're short a trainer now. What do you say, Charlie?"

Ashleigh looked over to the old man. His whole face lit up, but all he did was nod and say gruffly, "Be pleased to."

"Good," Townsend said. He laid a hand on Ashleigh's shoulder. "I'll sort out the details with your parents. Right now I imagine you want a few minutes alone with the filly.''

Ashleigh realized just how much she did. It was almost too much to absorb. Her parents were as stunned as she was when Mr. Townsend went to talk to them. Caroline, Rory, and Jilly were grinning like idiots. Linda was staring with her mouth open, but when Ashleigh approached, she rushed over and flung her arms around her friend. "I'm so happy for you!''

Mike was standing near Wonder. He and Terry had taken turns walking the filly during all the commotion. Ashleigh took one look at his face and smiled again. Terry patted Ashleigh's shoulder as he handed her the filly's lead shank. "Good going, kid. Everyone at the farm . . . well, nearly everyone . . . is going to be celebrating this!''

Ashleigh laughed. She reached up and hugged Wonder's neck. "You probably think we're all nuts, don't you girl? You just want to get back to your stall and eat. But what an incredible horse you are!''

Wonder nickered and affectionately nibbled Ashleigh's hair.

"Let's go, then,'' Ashleigh said with a sigh. Before she led the filly off, she glanced over to Mike. "Will you walk with us?''

"It would be an honor,'' he smiled as he fell into

step beside them. "What incredible news. I'm so happy for you. It probably hasn't sunk in yet."

Ashleigh gazed up at Wonder, who had her head between theirs, listening to every word. "It's beginning to . . . just a little."

"You'll make a great duo," Mike said.

Wonder immediately snorted and playfully nibbled Mike's sleeve.

"I think she's trying to tell you she wouldn't mind having you around, too." As soon as the words were out, Ashleigh blushed.

But Mike looked over and gave her the warmest smile. "I'd like that."

Wonder threw up her head, loudly whinnied her approval, and the three of them walked off to the backside.